Pe

Argum

Former Chairman of the Labour Party, the Fabian Society
and the Labour Home Policy Committee, Tony Benn has
held six ministerial posts in five Labour governments:
Postmaster-General in 1964, Minister of Technology in
1966, Minister of Power in 1969, Secretary of State for
Industry and Minister of Posts and Telecommunications
in 1974, and Energy Secretary from 1975 to 1979. His previous books include *The Regeneration of Britain*, *Speeches* and
Arguments for Democracy. He is the editor of *Writings on the
Wall: A Radical and Socialist Anthology 1215–1984* and the
author of numerous socialist pamphlets. Since 1950 he has
been elected twelve times as Member of Parliament for
Bristol South-East. He is now Member of Parliament for
Chesterfield.

Tony Benn

Arguments
for Socialism

Edited by Chris Mullin

Penguin Books

Penguin Books Ltd, Harmondsworth, Middlesex, England
Viking Penguin Inc., 40 West 23rd Street, New York, New York 10010, U.S.A.
Penguin Books Australia Ltd, Ringwood, Victoria, Australia
Penguin Books Canada Ltd, 2801 John Street, Markham, Ontario, Canada L3R 1B4
Penguin Books (N.Z.) Ltd, 182–190 Wairau Road, Auckland 10, New Zealand

—

First published by Jonathan Cape 1979
Published in Penguin Books 1980
Reprinted 1980 (twice), 1981, 1982, 1984, 1985

—

Copyright © Tony Benn, 1979
Introduction to the Penguin Edition
Copyright © Tony Benn, 1980
All rights reserved

—

Reproduced, printed and bound in Great Britain by
Cox & Wyman Ltd, Reading
Set in Monotype Baskerville

Dedicated with love and gratitude
to Caroline and the family

Contents

Editor's Note

Although we are said to have a free press in which a thousand flowers may bloom, a hundred schools of thought contend, the reality is different. There are in Britain today important points of view — held by large numbers of people — which cannot find serious and regular expression in our free press. For the most part this is true of democratic socialism of which Tony Benn is one of the most articulate exponents.

The central feature of political bias in the British media is not that the media necessarily support the Conservatives with a capital 'C', but they support the policies of conservatives with a small 'c' regardless of whether they are carried out by a Conservative or Labour government. The media also perform the additional service of comprehensively smearing as extremists those — like Tony Benn — whose principal offence is to call for the implementation of the Labour Party programme.

In Tony Benn's case the hysteria has been stimulated by the knowledge that, unlike many Labour politicians, he has both the ability and the will to put into practice the policy of the party. An all-time low was reached in the summer of 1975, during the massive and successful campaign to have him removed as Secretary of State for Industry: the *Daily Express* published his photograph daubed with a Hitler moustache (May 9th 1975); the *Daily Mail* — at that time engaged in one of its periodic mugging scare campaigns — ran an editorial headed 'Benn, the demon "mugger", unmasked' (July 31st 1975).

Arguments for Socialism puts the record straight and shows that there is a well-argued, reasonable case for a radical alternative approach to Britain's problems. A case which does not find adequate expression in our free press.

The first five sections of this book are based on speeches,

lectures and articles by Tony Benn taken mainly, but not exclusively, from the last five years. Some of the material was first brought together by Joan Bodington. My job has been, in consultation with Tony Benn, to reduce all this to a coherent narrative by removing repetition and outdated material; inserting notes and updating some of the statistics. The source material for each section is listed at the back of the book.

The final section — 'Issues for the 1980s' — was drawn from a long series of interviews.

May 1979   Chris Mullin

Introduction

Many books have been written about socialism, and some have had a profound influence on those who have read them. But the most important socialist teacher of all is experience.

Those of us in the British Labour Movement, looking back on the centuries of our history and tradition, will find that most of our own ideas were rooted in some event or series of events which radicalised contemporary thinking. All our greatest achievements—the building of trade unionism; the winning of the vote; the establishment of the Labour Party; its adoption of socialism; and the creation of the Welfare State—grew out of experience. Even today most people who think of themselves as Socialists can point to what has happened to them in their own lives which opened their minds to socialism.

And so it was with me. Some people begin life as socialists and end up in the House of Lords. In one sense I suppose I could be said to have done it the other way round. But the truth is, of course, very different.

I was confirmed an Anglican but brought up in a radical, dissenting and socialist tradition. My father, for twenty years a radical Liberal MP, joined the Labour Party and was elected as Labour MP for North Aberdeen when I was three. My mother, a Christian Socialist, is a life-long student of the Bible, and my earliest memories were of politics and religion, religion and politics, as the main subjects of discussion at home.

Though my family enjoyed a very comfortable standard of living and I was sent to Westminster School and on to Oxford, we were all committed to the Labour Party throughout the 1930s, and my own family today are all Socialists too.

I clearly remember the Tory landslide in 1931 when I was six, the Japanese invasion of Manchuria, the Abyssinian War, and Spain; and have copies of Labour's election literature which I distributed in the 1935 election, all of which we talked about at home. That manifesto was far more left wing — with its demand for the nationalisation of the Joint Stock Banks — than the Labour manifesto of 1979.

Though I walked over to Transport House to take out my first membership of the Labour Party on the birthday I became eligible to do so, in 1942, I was born into the Labour Movement, like millions of others, and I intend to be in it when I die.

In 1942, at the age of sixty-five, Father — like many Labour MPs and ex-Labour Cabinet ministers — was put into the House of Lords. He moved steadily to the Left in his thinking as he got older and reflected on his experience of life, arguing for world peace, human rights and civil liberties. Indeed, in that, as in so many other ways, my life has followed the pattern of his.

The menace of fascism first became real for me when as a child I saw Sir Oswald Mosley strutting through the streets of London with his uniformed men in their black shirts; and I was with Father on the platform at an East End Labour meeting which the Blackshirts tried to break up. The ranting voice of Hitler, heard over the BBC at a Nuremberg rally, somehow brought the inevitability of war home more clearly even than the newsreels from Spain or the attack on Austria.

Later, in the RAF, on a troopship to Africa to train as a pilot in 1944, and returning in 1945 from the Middle East on another troopship full of men from the 'forgotten army' in Burma — and on every occasion that presented itself in between — we talked about politics and the post-war world.

My brother Michael — killed in 1944 on active service as a night fighter pilot — and I corresponded about socialism and religion by airletter and aerogramme. And when in 1944 in Rhodesia I visited a hospital with a European nurse, whose family had befriended me, and saw the absolutely appalling conditions of squalor under which the Africans were treated, within a stone's throw of a well-equipped modern hospital for white patients, I was deeply stirred.

It was all this which later drew me to great Socialists like

Fenner Brockway, from whom I learned so much and with whom I worked as a founder member of the Movement for Colonial Freedom and in organising the national petition against the hydrogen bomb in 1955.

One radicalising experience was of minor personal importance to anyone but me. It was my attempt to renounce the peerage that devolved on me as his heir when Father died in 1960 — after my elder brother Michael's death — Father having been made a peer before the days of life peerages. That struggle taught me more about the British establishment and how it really works, and how to defeat it, than any other episode in my life.

Both the Lords and the Commons threw out Renunciation Bills that I had introduced. They were very polite about it, but saw that any breach in the hereditary principle could undermine a significant part of the buttress supporting their privileges and power.

So, when Father died, though I had been an MP for ten years, elected four times by Bristol South East, I was expelled from the Commons without even a hearing at the Bar. A by-election was declared to choose my successor. My local Labour Party re-adopted me, at once, as their Labour candidate and the electors sent me back to the Commons with a hugely increased majority as their new MP.

The House would not admit me, and I was hauled before two judges, sitting as an election court, which had to adjudicate on the validity of my election. These two judges were courteous and considerate to a fault. I deployed my own legal case based upon ancient precedents and the more commonsense view that, in 1961, service as an elected MP should have priority over the feudal nonsense of a hereditary title. But the two judges were unmoved, and they unseated me, basing their judgment on a statement by Mr Justice Dodderidge in 1626, that a peerage was an 'incorporeal hereditament affixed in the blood and annexed to the posterity'. The court then declared my defeated opponent to be the rightful MP for Bristol South East, and he took his seat in the Commons in my place, and I was sent a bill for £5,000 to pay the legal fees of the two QCs he had engaged.

But the anger of my constituents at this absurd denial of their democratic rights triggered off such a public reaction that the Macmillan Government was forced to introduce legislation to permit peers to renounce, which I did within five minutes of the Bill becoming law in 1963. This battle, and the victory we won, taught me lessons about the British class system, the role of the courts, and the countervailing power of the people, if aroused, that I shall never forget.

Unusually, it gave me, who had never experienced any hardships in life, just enough of a taste of what happens when authority decides to crush a dissident. From that moment on, both as an MP and as a minister, I saw through completely new eyes, and understood, the experiences of all those who really suffered from far more serious abuses directed against them by those enjoying authority deriving from wealth, or status, or power. It was a very strange way to learn a basic lesson, but everyone learns best from his own experience.

Nowhere is that abuse of wealth and power more nakedly obvious than in our industrial system under modern British capitalism. First, as Minister of Technology, and later as Secretary of State for Industry, I met tens of thousands of skilled and unskilled workers whose legal status in relation to their employer was little better than high-grade serfdom. They could be hired and fired almost at will, their factories sold, or closed, or merged, or cut back, and the workers had no rights to be consulted or even to be told the facts that led their employers to sack them.

I believe that the class system in industry is the root cause of most industrial unrest in Britain today. Bad industrial relations cannot be blamed upon a few thoughtful Socialists who are vilified by the mass media as wreckers or extremists.

It may also seem strange that a Cabinet minister should be radicalised while in office. It would be more usual for a radical MP to be converted to respectability the moment that he receives his Seals of Office. For me it was different. The shipyard workers who organised the work-in at Upper Clyde Shipbuilders, the brave men and women who fought so hard to set up Meriden and Kirkby Manufacturing and Engineering as co-operatives, and the brilliant and humane shop stewards at Lucas Aerospace combined with hundreds of others to give me an education in the real meaning of practical socialism which no books or teachers could have matched.

The Labour Party's 1974 election manifestos contained policies that had been fully worked out to open up a really new vision of industrial life that would have transformed the situation in a decade. But it was at that point that another lesson had to be learned.

I discovered how the immense power of the bankers and the industrialists in Britain, and world-wide, could be used to bring direct and indirect pressure, again backed by the media, first to halt, and then to reverse, the policy of a Labour Government that both the electors and the House of Commons had accepted.

I had also to learn that ex-Imperial Britain was now apparently meekly accepting the status of a colony or protectorate, whose economic policy was dictated by the International Monetary Fund; whose industrial policy by the multinationals; whose foreign and defence policy was integrated with NATO; and whose statutes were only legal if they did not breach the provisions of the Treaty of Rome as interpreted and administered by non-elected officials in Brussels known as the Common Market Commissioners.

Those, then, were some of the experiences which have led me to a clearer understanding of—and commitment to—a socialism that is open, libertarian, pluralistic, humane and democratic.

Anyone who has the opportunity of studying that rich tradition will soon discover it has nothing whatever in common with the harsh, centralised, dictatorial and mechanistic images of socialism which are purposely presented by our opponents and a tiny group of people who control the mass media in Britain today.

But, despite all these problems, the message of socialism does get through, and in time experience will encourage more and more people to ask questions about it; and then to come to understand that it offers a better way forward for us and our children.

I hope that some who read these pages will find a few passages that will encourage them to question their own condition, discuss their experience with others, and then work to bring about the reforms needed to allow us all to lead fuller, richer, and more creative lives.

Introduction
to the Penguin Edition

1979 marked the end of the consensus, based on full employment and the welfare state, which had dominated British politics since the war.

This consensus rested upon a high level of economic activity born out of rearmament, and sustained by the needs of reconstruction and the growth of world trade. So secure did the boom appear to be at its peak in the late fifties that Conservative leaders were able to proclaim the birth of a new liberal capitalism that could promise plenty for all; and some Labour leaders, in response, began to speak of socialism and the traditional role of trade unionism as if they were out of date and in need of revision.

But during the sixties, a nagging anxiety returned, as Britain's underlying weaknesses began to threaten the false promise of continuing growth. The Keynesian analysis which underpinned consensus optimism was attacked from a new Left inspired by the events of 1968; and by a new Right which rallied round the rediscovered philosophy of monetarism.

Thus, during the 1970s, British politics began to come to life again, as real arguments about real policy choices broke through the façade of ritualised parliamentary exchanges about which leadership could run the system best.

OPEC oil price increases, pressure from the IMF and the multinationals, and from the EEC, and the resurgence of active trade unionism, especially on the shopfloor, were real events external to the House of Commons, and not easy to accommodate within the framework of an uncritical bipartisan faith in the moral supremacy of a mixed economy, run by men of goodwill.

The more consensus politics came under external attack, the more the establishment began to huddle together and the more they were drawn to corporatist solutions to be worked out at the top and imposed by law or coercion. But consensus corporatism has no popular constituency of its own. Insofar as it involved planning to defend a weakened industry, it could not satisfy the needs of capital; and insofar as it presented state capitalism as if it were socialism, it failed to satisfy the aspirations of Labour.

The defeat of Labour in 1970, of the Conservatives twice in 1974, and of Labour again in 1979, effectively signalled public disenchantment with all attempts to prolong policies that had outlived their usefulness and their effectiveness.

It was this policy void that the new Conservative leadership exploited with boldness and skill in the closing years of the seventies. And, in parallel with this, the Labour Party and the Labour Movement began to rediscover their vision and their socialist role — muted only by the need to sustain a Labour Cabinet in power.

The speeches in this book were all delivered from within that Labour Cabinet, with all the limitations which that involved. They necessarily related mainly to the matters with which, as a departmental minister, I was directly involved, presented wherever possible within a wider perspective, so as to open up the real issues involved.

In that sense they were designed to help the Labour Movement to appreciate the need for socialism and to understand its roots, its relevance, and its future constitution.

The 1980s will see those arguments developed more plainly, more openly, and more urgently. Polarisation that monetarism has induced cannot be neutralised by a return to the stale policies of consensus. Monetarism is divisive and immoral, as well as being destined to failure. Indeed, its greatest danger is that it could lead to a new and harsher authoritarianism of the Right.

If that is to be avoided, the democratic socialist case has got to be presented with clarity, humanity, urgency and courage.

The political arguments we shall be witnessing in the 1980s are real and important, and we must shape our society by building upon what is best in our inheritance and adding to it a true vision of what we are capable of achieving.

That is what this book is all about.

January 1980

THE INHERITANCE

I

The Inheritance of the Labour Movement

The British Labour Movement draws its inspiration from a history that goes back over many centuries. This movement arose directly from the twin struggles by the British people to control Parliament through the popular vote and to gain the right to organise free trade unions. The battles against the Combination Acts and similar legislation which made trade unionism illegal went hand in hand with the campaigns for working men and women to be represented in Parliament. But even before these historic struggles, which first saw the light of day in the industrial revolution, the origins of socialism can be traced back as far as the time of Christ himself and even to the Old Testament.

Today it is frequently said that the Labour Party is moving further to the left than can be justified by its origins. This is not so and, to illustrate the point, I have selected and amplified a number of the more important trains of thought and action from which the origins of the Labour Movement in Britain can be traced. Those I have chosen are the Bible, the seventeenth-century Levellers, the work of Karl Marx and the Labour Party's own Constitution.

Christianity and Socialism

Critics often seek to dismiss socialism as being necessarily atheistical. But this is not true as far as British socialism is concerned. For the Bible has always been, and remains, a

23

major element in our national political — as well as our religious — education. And within our movement Christian Socialists have played an important role, along with Humanists, Marxists, Fabians and Co-operators. The conflict in the Old Testament between the Kings and the Prophets — between temporal power and the preaching of righteousness — has greatly affected our own ideas about society; and of course lay at the heart of both arguments in the English Revolution, the one between the King and Parliament, and the other between Cromwell and the Levellers.

For example, in the Bible, it was the prophet Micah who proclaimed this message from God:

> He hath shewed thee, O man, what is good; and what doth the Lord require of thee, but to do justly, and to love mercy, and to walk humbly with thy God?
>
> (Micah Ch.6,v.8)

The deep conviction to be found in the Old Testament that conscience is God-given, or derives from nature or reason, and must be supreme over man-made law, has its origins in these Bible teachings, and is still passionately held today.

Later, when Jesus Christ, the Carpenter of Nazareth, was asked by one of the scribes, 'What commandment is the first of all?' St Mark's Gospel, Ch. 12, vv. 29–31, records his answer:

> 'The first ... is, Hear O Israel; The Lord our God is one Lord:
> And thou shalt love the Lord thy God with all thy heart, and with all thy soul, and with all thy strength ...
> The second is like, namely this, Thou shalt love thy neighbour as thyself. There is none other commandment greater than these.'

Jesus's classic restatement of the Old Testament teaching of monotheism, and of brotherly love under one God which flowed from it, was absolutely revolutionary when uttered in a world which still accepted slavery. This passage also underlines the idea of man's relationship with God as a person-to-person relationship, neither needing, nor requiring us to accept, the intervention of an exclusive priestly class claiming a monopoly right to speak on behalf of the Almighty, still less of a king claiming a divine right to rule.

These ideas lie at the root of religious dissent, and gave birth to the idea of the priesthood of all believers which is central to non-conformity. H. G. Wells, himself a non-believer, writing of Jesus in his *History of the World*, recognised the revolutionary nature of Christ's teachings which led to his crucifixion.[1]

> In view of what he plainly said, is it any wonder that all who were rich and prosperous felt a horror of strange things, a swimming of their world at his teaching? He was dragging out all the little private reservations they had made from social service into the light of a universal religious life. He was like some terrible moral huntsman digging mankind out of the smug burrows in which they had lived hitherto. In the white blaze of this kingdom of his there was to be no property, no privilege, no pride and precedence; no motive indeed and no reward but love. Is it any wonder that men were dazzled and blinded and cried out against him? Even his disciples cried out when he would not spare them the light. Is it any wonder that the priests realised that between this man and themselves there was no choice but that he or priestcraft should perish? Is it any wonder that the Roman soldiers, confronted and amazed by something soaring over their comprehension and threatening all their disciplines, should take refuge in wild laughter and crown him with thorns and robe him in purple and make a mock Caesar out of him? For to take him seriously was to enter upon a strange and alarming life, to abandon habits, to control instincts and impulses, to essay an incredible happiness.

Wells's words must rank as one of the most remarkable tributes to Christ ever to have come from a non-Christian.

No wonder that many bishops and clergy in England before the Reformation feared that the Bible—if available to be read widely—might undermine the priestly hold over the minds of their flock. They therefore punished those like Wycliffe and the Lollards who translated the Bible into English and encouraged people to read it, thus undermining the authority of the bishops and the priesthood, the King and the landlords.

The *History of Oxfordshire* tells us of a Lollard who paid £1 for an English Bible so that he could read it with his friends, many of them weavers. They were forced to kneel on the altar steps in Burford Church, throughout the whole of morning service, with faggots on their shoulders. These faggots were no doubt burned to heat the branding irons with which this group of Bible readers, twelve men and nine women, were all branded on the cheek at the end of prayers, to teach the congregation not to read the Bible.[2] For then, as now, in many parts of the world the Bible was seen as a revolutionary book not to be trusted to the common people to read and interpret for themselves. No wonder then that the Levellers should regard the Bible as their basic text. Leveller pamphlets abound with religious quotations. Divine teaching, as they read it, expressly prohibited the domination of man by man.

One historian summarised the views being advanced by the lower classes at the beginning of the Civil War. This is what was being said, for example, in Chelmsford — and very radical it was:[3]

The relation of Master and Servant has no ground in the New Testament; in Christ there is neither bond nor free. Ranks such as those of the peerage and gentry are 'ethnical and heathenish distinctions'. There is no ground in nature or Scripture why one man should have £1000 per annum, another not £1. The common people have been kept under blindness and ignorance, and have remained servants and slaves to the nobility and gentry. But God hath now opened their eyes and discovered unto them their Christian liberty.

The Diggers, or True Levellers[4] as they described themselves, went even further and in Gerard Winstanley's pamphlet *The True Levellers' Standard Advanced*, published on April 26th 1649, these words appear that anticipated the conservationists and commune dwellers of today, that denounced the domination of man by man, proclaimed the equality of women and based it all on God and Nature's laws:[5]

In the beginning of Time, the great Creator, Reason, made the earth to be a Common Treasury, to preserve Beasts, Birds, Fishes and Man, the Lord that was to govern this Creation; for Man had Domination given to him, over the Beasts, Birds and Fishes; but not one word was spoken in the beginning, that one branch of mankind should rule over another.

And the reason is this, every single man, Male and Female, is a perfect creature of himself; and the same Spirit that made the Globe dwells in man to govern the Globe; so that the flesh of man being subject to Reason, his Maker, hath him to be his Teacher and Ruler within himself, therefore needs not to run abroad after any Teacher and Ruler without him, for he needs not that any man should teach him, for the same Anoynting that ruled in the Son of Man, teacheth him all things.

But since human flesh (that king of Beasts) began to delight himself in the objects of Creation, more than in the Spirit Reason and Righteousness ... Covetousness, did set up one man to teach and rule over another; and thereby the Spirit was killed, and man was brought into bondage and became a greater Slave to such of his own kind, than the Beasts of the field were to him.

And hereupon the Earth (which was made to be a Common Treasury for relief for all, both Beasts and Men) was hedged in to Inclosures by the teachers and rulers, and the others were made Servants and Slaves; And that Earth that is within this Creation made a Common Store-house for all, is bought and sold, and kept in the hands of a few, whereby the great Creator is mightily dishonoured, as if he were a respecter of persons, delighting in the comfortable livelihood of some, and rejoycing in the miserable povertie and straits of others. From the beginning it was not so.

The plain advocacy of absolute human equality—and the emphasis on the common ownership of land and natural resources—speaks to us today with the same power as when those words were written by Winstanley.

The Bridge between Christianity and Socialism

But some Levellers went beyond the authority of the Bible and began to develop out of it, and from their own experience, a humanist buttress for their social philosophy without losing its moral force. They were, in a special sense, bridge-builders; constructing a bridge that connects Christian teaching with humanism and democratic socialism.

Those who crossed that bridge did not blow it up behind them as converts to atheism might have done. That bridge is still there for anyone who wishes to cross it in either direction. Some use it to go back to trace one of the paths leading to the Bible. Others like the modern Christian pilgrims — for example the Catholic priests and others in Latin America — whose experience of modern world poverty, persecution and oppression has spurred them on to cross that same bridge from Christianity to social action and democratic socialism, have based it on their Christian faith, and the inspiration of saintly Christians who have pioneered along the same path.

The moral force of Bible teaching, and the teachings of Jesus, are not necessarily weakened by being secularised. Indeed, it can be argued that humanism may entrench them more strongly, for those who cannot accept the Christian faith.

Christians believe that the Almighty created man to be his children and that the brotherhood of man, under God, is the basis of all social morality, and the divine source of authority for it. Humanists, by contrast, accepting the brotherhood of man as a deeply felt experience, explain the idea of a Divine Father as deriving from man's desire to embody his highest aspirations of social morality in that reverent way through a Personal God. Though these beliefs stand in blank opposition to each other theologically, many Christians, humanists and secular socialists are, in practice, committed to a code of human ethics that is intended to be identical in its application to society, however far below this ideal man may fall in practice. But however we choose to explain this theological paradox, Christian, humanist and socialist moralities have in fact co-existed and co-operated throughout history and they co-exist and co-operate today most fruitfully and not only within the

Christian Socialist movement itself. The British trade union and Labour Movement, like Anglicans, Presbyterians, Catholics, Methodists, Congregationalists, Baptists, Jews and campaigners for civil rights have all gained inspiration from these twin traditions of Christianity and humanistic socialism.

We should certainly not allow the horrors of persecution committed at various times in history by societies proclaiming themselves to be Christian to blind us to the true teachings of Christ. Nor should we allow the horrors of persecution committed more recently by societies claiming to be socialist to blind us to the true social morality of socialism.

The Levellers and the English Democratic Tradition[6]

The issues raised in the historic conflict between Charles I, resting his claim to govern Britain on the Divine Right of Kings, and Parliament represented — albeit imperfectly — a demand for the wider sharing of power. They remain alive in British politics to this day because they concern the use, and abuse, of state power, which is a subject of universal and continuing relevance. The Levellers grew out of the conditions of their own time. They represented the aspirations of working people who suffered under the persecution of kings, landowners and the priestly class and they spoke for those who experienced the hardships of poverty and deprivation. The Levellers developed and campaigned, first with Cromwell and then against him, for a political and constitutional settlement of the Civil War which would embody principles of political freedom that anticipated by a century and a half the main idea of the American and French Revolutions. Their advocacy of democracy and equality has been taken up by generations of liberal and socialist thinkers and activists, pressing for reforms, many of which are still strongly contested in this country to this day. The Levellers can now be seen, not only as having played a major role in their own period, but as speaking for a popular liberation movement which can be traced right back to the teachings of the Bible, which has retained its vitality in the intervening centuries and which speaks to us today with undiminished force. The Levellers developed their own traditions of free discussion and vigorous petitioning, and used them to formulate and advance their own demands.

These demands included the drafting of a major document called 'The Agreement of the People' which outlined a new and democratic constitution for Britain. The preamble to the third draft, published on May 1st 1649, runs as follows:[7]

> We, the free People of England, to whom God hath given hearts, means and opportunity to effect the same, do with submission to his wisdom, in his name, and desiring the equity thereof may be to his praise and glory; Agree to ascertain our Government to abolish all arbitrary Power, and to set bounds and limits both to our Supreme, and all Subordinate Authority, and remove all known Grievances. And accordingly do declare and publish to all the world, that we are agreed as followeth,
>
> 1. That the Supreme Authority of England and the Territories therewith incorporate, shall be and reside henceforth in a Representative of the people consisting of four hundred persons, but no more; in the choice of whom (according to natural right) all men of the age of one and twenty years and upwards (not being servants, or receiving alms, or having served the late King in Arms or voluntary Contributions), shall have their voices.

The Levellers held themselves to be free-born Englishmen, entitled to the protection of a natural law of human rights which they believed to originate in the will of God, rights vested in the people to whom alone true sovereignty belonged. These sovereign rights, the Levellers maintained, were only loaned to Parliament, who, having been elected on a wide popular franchise, would hold them in trust. The Levellers also believed passionately in religious toleration and rejected oppression by presbyters as much as by priests, wishing to end the horrific record of executions, burnings, brandings and banishments that Christians had perpetrated on themselves and others, that had led to the martyrdom of thousands of good Catholics and Protestants, dissenters, Jews and gentiles alike.

The rank and file within the New Model Army[8] spoke

through Adjutants, Agents or Agitators (hence the special odium attaching to that word in the British establishment to this day) who wore the sea-green colours that are still associated with incorruptibility. They demanded and won—for a time—democratic control of the Armed Forces and secured equal representation on a Grand Council of the Army, sharing decisions with the generals and colonels, known to them as the Grandees. They regarded the Normans as oppressors of England and the King as the symbol of that Conquest who was buttressed and supported by land-owners who had seized much land once held in common, land that they argued should be restored to common ownership.

They argued for universal state schools and hospitals to be provided at public expense three centuries before our generation began, so painfully, to construct the Welfare State, the National Health Service and the comprehensive school system against so much resistance.

The Levellers distilled their political philosophy by discussion out of their own experience, mixing theory and practice, thought and action, and by doing so they passed on to succeeding generations a formula for social progress from which we can learn how to tackle the problems of our time. The Levellers won wide support among the people as a whole; and though Cromwell and his generals ultimately defeated them, their ideas still retain a special place in the political traditions of the people of England.

Looking back on these ideas from the vantage point of the present, and knowing that they came out of the minds and experience of working people, few of whom enjoyed the formal education available today, we can imagine the intense excitement and the controversy that those demands must have created when they were first formulated. It is also a real comfort for us to discover that, in our present social, political, human and industrial struggles, we are the inheritors of such a strong and ancient tradition of action and analysis.

The ideas of the Levellers were thought to be so dangerous because of their popularity that the establishment wanted to silence them. By 1650 the Levellers' movement had been effectively crushed. Cromwell's Commonwealth represented a formidable advance compared to the reign of King Charles which preceded it. But it did not — and in terms of its historical and industrial development probably could not — adopt the principles that the Levellers were advocating. Ten years later came the Restoration of Charles II. In 1688 Britain witnessed the shadowy beginnings of a constitutional monarchy which, as it emerged at that time, had practically nothing whatever in common with political democracy.

But the elimination of the Levellers as an organised political movement could not obliterate their ideas. From that day to this the same principles of religious and political freedom and equality have reappeared again and again in the history of the Labour Movement and throughout the world.

The American colonists inscribed these principles clearly in their Declaration of Independence issued by the Congress on July 4th 1776:

> We hold these Truths to be self-evident, that all Men are created equal, that they are endowed by their Creator with certain inalienable Rights, that among these are Life, Liberty and the Pursuit of Happiness. That to secure these Rights, Governments are instituted among Men deriving their just Powers from the Consent of the Governed.

The document was drafted by our American cousins but the ideas were taken straight from the British Levellers a century and a quarter before.

The Americans had also drawn heavily on the writings of Tom Paine, who was a direct heir of the Leveller traditions; and whose *Rights of Man* also won him a place in the history of the French Revolution where, though English, he was elected as a Deputy to the first French Constituent Assembly summoned to implement the principles of Liberty, Equality and Fraternity. The English reformers of the early nineteenth century also drew many of their ideas from that mysterious mix of Christian teaching, religious and political dissent, social equality and democracy. This fired the imagination of generations of Congregationalists, trade union pioneers, early Co-operators, Socialists, and the Chartists who also used language the Levellers themselves might have spoken. 'Brother Chartists,' began one leaflet, issued by the Executive Committee of the National Chartist Association in 1842:

> The great Political Truths which have been agitated during the last half-century, have at length aroused the degraded and insulted White Slaves of England, to a sense of their duty to themselves, their children and their country. Tens of thousands have flung down their implements of labour. Your taskmasters tremble at your energy, and expecting masses eagerly watch this great crisis of our cause.
>
> Labour must no longer be the common prey of masters and rulers. Intelligence has beamed upon the mind of the bondsman, and he has been convinced that all wealth, comfort and produce, everything valuable, useful, and elegant, have sprung from the palm of his hand; he feels that his cottage is empty, his back thinly clad, his children breadless, himself hopeless, his mind harassed, and his body punished, that undue riches, luxury and gorgeous plenty might be heaped in the palaces of the taskmasters, and flooded into the granaries of the oppressor. Nature, God, and Reason have condemned this inequality, and in the thunder of a people's voice it must perish for ever.

We can find the same aspirations in the moving words of Clause IV of the Labour Party Constitution (which we shall shortly be considering), written in 1918, which aims 'to secure for the workers by hand or by brain the full fruits of their industry ... ' The same ideas were expressed in Labour's 1973 Programme for Britain, which spoke of bringing about 'a fundamental and irreversible shift in the balance of wealth and power in favour of working people and their families'. A very significant expression of these sentiments was that made by Karl Marx.

Marxism and the Labour Party[9]

Marxism has, from the earliest days, always been openly accepted by the Labour Party as one of many sources of inspiration within the Labour Movement along with — though much less influential than — Christian socialism, Fabianism, Owenism, trade unionism, or even radical liberalism.

The party has, of course, consistently opposed the admission of those who belong to other parties calling themselves socialists, where these parties have put up candidates to oppose official Labour candidates in local or parliamentary elections. This has automatically ruled out the admission of members of the Communist Party, which, in addition to its disqualification on these grounds, has for a long period condoned violations of human rights in the USSR and Eastern Europe under Stalin and others; and even supported the use of Soviet troops against Hungary and other independent countries in the past. But never since the earliest days of the Labour Movement has Marxism itself been regarded as a disqualification for party membership.

All that is required by way of political allegiance from party members, or paid officials, is that they should accept the policy and programme of the Labour Party and thus commit themselves to advancing socialism through parliamentary democracy. This is a position many are determined to maintain.

The Labour Party has been, is, and always will be an extremely tolerant and undogmatic party, deriving much strength and popular support from its refusal to impose a rigid test of doctrine upon its members. The influences that lead individuals to embrace democratic socialism have always been left to the individual conscience, and there are no inquisitions to root out Marxists any more than there are to root out Catholics, atheists, or followers of Adam Smith, Sigmund Freud, Leon Trotsky or Milton Friedman.

It is, however, important that the Labour Party's attitude to Marxism should be restated at a time when the Tory Party, and the Tory press, are campaigning hard to persuade the British people that the Labour Party is dominated by Marxists (which it is not), that Marxism and Communism are synonymous (which they are not), and that there is a dominant group growing up within the Labour Party which really believes in violent revolution and the suppression of democratic rights, and the introduction of a one-party state (which there is not).

Perhaps the classic text is to be found in *The Labour Party in Perspective* written by Clem Attlee in 1937.[10] Attlee described the Marxist contribution to the Party in these words:

The ideas which called the pioneers to the service of the Socialist Movement were very varied. They were not the followers of a single gospel of one prophet. They did not accept one revelation as inspired. It is this which distinguishes the British Socialist Movement from many of those on the Continent.

Predominantly, the parties on the Continent have been built on the writings of Karl Marx. Around his teachings the Movement has grown. Different interpretations have been put upon his creed. In some countries other powerful influences have been at work and the characters of his apostles and the circumstances of the countries to which they belong have necessarily caused differences in the method pursued by particular parties, but they have this in common — that they were formed as definite Socialist movements, inspired by the word revealed to Marx.

In Britain the history of the Movement has been entirely different. Widely diffused as his influence has been, the number of those who accepted Marxism as a creed has always been small. The number of those who have entered the Socialist Movement as a direct result of his teaching has been but a fraction of the whole.

One must seek the inspiration of the majority of British Socialists in other directions.

There were, however, three organisations which have been the main contributors to the spread of Socialist thought in this country, and to the creation of a political Socialist Movement. All three have their own characteristics.

The first was the Social Democratic Federation. Founded by H. M. Hyndman, it was based definitely on the teaching of Karl Marx.

In 1943 Harold Laski wrote a pamphlet under the title *Marx and Today*.[11] In it, Laski, who was a member of the National Executive Committee of the party and its Chairman two years later, identified himself as a Marxist.

The view I am anxious to urge in this essay is the simple one that, in the light of the character of our age, the future of the British Labour Movement depends upon two things. It depends, first, upon our ability to recognise the bankruptcy of the traditional horror of principles by which it has been permeated; and granted the understanding of that bankruptcy, it depends, secondly, upon our willingness to adapt the essentials of the Marxist philosophy to the situation we occupy.

Laski went on to write:[12]

What do we mean today by a Marxist basis? Sixty years after Marx's death, it would be foolish to pretend that Marxism is a body of sacred formulas, the mere incantation of which charms away our danger; Marx himself would have been the first to admit the immense addition to our knowledge since he wrote, the urgency of taking full account of what that new knowledge implies in the fullest perspective we can give it.

And later still, in his pamphlet, Laski wrote:[13]

The preservation of individuality, its extension, indeed, its ability to affirm its own essence, that is, I believe, the central aim of any ethic that Marxism can endorse.

Over the years a very large number of members of the party, including some of our most distinguished leaders, have been drawn to socialism by study of Marx. Leaving aside entirely those who have left the Communist Party in order to join the Labour Party, there are many others whose Marxism led them into the Labour Party.

Herbert Morrison was one of the most famous. In a recent biography, Morrison's early experience and opinions were set out quite clearly:[14]

Morrison put a revolutionary Marxist line, liberally spiced with quotations from Marx, whose first volume of *Capital* he brought with him to the meetings. Indeed, he took a *Capital* almost everywhere at this time ...

Thus Morrison's biographers describe his early radical days in 1908. But they go on to tell how he became dissatisfied with the SDF as a vehicle to achieve his objective:[15] 'He first began to move away from it for tactical reasons. He wanted it to affiliate to the Labour Party, so as to permeate it with Marxist ideas.' Herbert Morrison believed therefore that Marxists should join the Labour Party in order to influence its policy. But, like many others before him, and since, his views were later tempered by the experience of working within the mainstream of the movement.

Michael Foot, in his biography of Aneurin Bevan, describes a dinner which he attended with Nye Bevan in Soho in 1952, held at a restaurant where Karl Marx had once found sanctuary:[16]

> At the beginning of the proceedings we drank a toast to the great man's memory and there was no sign then — or at any other time, for that matter, in my knowledge of him — that Bevan wished to disown his debt to Marxism, so long, of course, as the doctrine was undogmatically interpreted.

Indeed, an interest in Marxism has by no means been confined to the present Left of the Labour Party. In a letter published in *Tribune* Tony Crosland wrote as follows:[17]

> We conceive the function of *Tribune* to be the expression in popular form, and to as large a public as possible, of the views of the Left and Marxist wing of social democracy in this country. Its policy must be that of those who believe that the present leadership of the Labour Party is not sufficiently socialist ...

The contribution made by Marx to social democracy is widely recognised and admired by those who would not wish to call themselves Marxists. In a letter dated March 17th 1972 to Willy Brandt of Germany and Bruno Kreisky of Austria, Olaf Palme, then Prime Minister of Sweden, has this to say:[18]

> I have always found it difficult to understand why elitist thinkers and supporters of revolutionary violence should regard themselves as the standard bearers of a Socialist and Marxist tradition which has its roots in Western Europe and in Western European humanism.

Indeed, though it should not be necessary to have to emphasise this, the role and contribution that Karl Marx has made has been widely recognised by those who would not call themselves socialist at all. For example, in his book *A Religion for Agnostics* Professor Nathaniel Micklem, the distinguished Congregational preacher and former Principal of Mansfield College, writes:[19] 'Though he disguised his moral indignation under cover of scientific terminology, it was in response to the call of a higher and more lasting justice that Karl Marx repudiated the "bourgeois" inequality of his day.' It is not only in the West that Marxism is seen as one of the main sources of democratic socialist philosophy. Marxists have been amongst the sternest critics of the Soviet control in Eastern Europe. In Czechoslovakia in 1968 the famous 'Prague Spring' was inspired and led by men who declared themselves to be Marxists. For example, in a lecture given by Ivan Svitak at the Charles University of Prague on May 3rd 1968, the following passage appeared:

> Marx was not, is not, and will never be, the inventor and theoretician of totalitarian dictatorship that he appears today, when the original meaning of his work — true humanism — has been given a thoroughly Byzantine and Asian twist.
>
> Marx strove for a wider humanism than that of the bourgeois democracies that he knew, and for wider civil rights, not for the setting up of the dictatorship of one class and one political party.
>
> What is today thought to be the Marxist theory of the state and Marxist social science is simply an ideological forgery, a false, contemporary conception, as wrong as the idea that the orbits of heavenly bodies are circular ...
>
> By contrast, the faithful, historical picture of the real Marx shows the scholar, the European, the democrat, the socialist, the tribune of the people, the humanist, the revolutionary, the internationalist, the giant personality and the messenger of freedom.

The approach to Marxism contained in these quotations may help to explain why even those non-Marxists, who, like myself, are not part of that Marxist tradition, firmly believe that a place for those who are must be preserved within the Labour Movement—in exactly the same way, and for exactly the same reasons, as for all other streams of thought.

Karl Marx, who worked and wrote in England and about the English working class, has long been recognised in Britain as a towering socialist philosopher who brought methods of scientific analysis to a study of society and we certainly rank him with the greatest minds in history, along with Copernicus, Darwin, Freud and Einstein. It would be as wrong to blame him for Stalin's tyranny as it would be to lay blame for the Spanish Inquisition on the teachings of Jesus. Marx and Engels, Rosa Luxemburg and Trotsky, together with a whole range of foreign socialist philosophers, have been read by British socialists as we have developed our own home-grown beliefs in freedom, democracy and equality, and this is reflected in the Constitution of the Labour Party.

Clause IV

At its 1918 Conference, the Labour Party officially adopted socialism as its objective and the Constitution contained within it the famous Clause IV which set out that commitment to language that still speaks to us today with the force that it commanded then. Clause IV is often referred to but rarely quoted in full. It remains the clearest and best possible statement of the democratic, socialist faith and below I have set it out in full:[20]

Clause IV—Party Objects

1 To organise and maintain in Parliament and in the country a Political Labour Party.

2 To co-operate with the General Council of the Trades Union Congress, or other Kindred Organisations, in joint political or other action in harmony with the Party Constitution and Standing Orders.

3 To give effect as far as may be practicable to the principles from time to time approved by the Party Conference.

4 To secure for the workers by hand or by brain the full fruits of their industry and the most equitable distribution thereof that may be possible upon the basis of the common

ownership of the means of production, distribution, and exchange, and the best obtainable system of popular administration and control of each industry or service.

5 Generally to promote the Political, Social and Economic Emancipation of the People, and more particularly of those who depend directly upon their own exertions by hand or by brain for the means of life.

6 To co-operate with the Labour and Socialist organisations in the Commonwealth Overseas with a view to promoting the purposes of the Party, and to take common action for the promotion of a higher standard of social and economic life for the working population of the respective countries.

7 To co-operate with the Labour and Socialist organisations in other countries and to support the United Nations Organisation ... for the promotion of peace, the adjustment and settlement of international disputes by conciliation or judicial arbitration, the establishment and defence of human rights, and the improvement of the social and economic standards and conditions of work of the people of the world.

Clause IV is so important that each of its seven paragraphs deserves some sort of commentary.

Paragraph One states the clear commitment of the party to democratic change through Parliament and sets out the requirement to organise a political movement to win support for its candidates for that purpose.

Paragraph Two spells out the objective of maintaining a close and continuing relationship with the Trades Union Congress and other organisations which will assist in realising the aims of the party.

Paragraph Three lays down the role of the party conference and its relationship to the party in Parliament. This key paragraph differentiates the Labour Party from all other parties in Britain because it gives individual members in the constituencies and affiliated members through the trades unions the right to decide the principles of policy through their delegates at conference. It also calls upon the National Executive, the parliamentary party and Labour ministers in office to implement these policies 'as far as may be practicable'. It does not, as is often asserted, seek to transfer the responsibility of government, when Labour is in power, from Parliament to Conference. But it is intended to mean, and must mean, that Labour leaders must accept their obligation to carry out policies decided by the rank and file and not to regard those activists who make up the real movement in the country as a mere fan club for the political leadership—endorsing all they say and do uncritically, and limited in their role to offering advice that can be rejected or accepted at will by the top brass of the party. This provision in the Constitution is the hinge that joins the people to their party and it must be seen as a crucial element in the commitment of the party to democratic change. For without it those who join and work for the party and thus help to win power for a Labour government would have no guarantee whatsoever that their efforts would secure the changes which led them to join the party. The leadership of the party can be seen, therefore, to share a collective responsibility with the party rank and file to carry out the programme settled by Conference and presented to the electorate in the Manifesto.

Paragraph Four contains the best known and most quoted words. The idea of securing for the workers 'the full fruits of their industry' owes much to the concept of a 'surplus' appropriated from labour for capital which embodies the moral appeal of the Labour theory of value. This does not, as is often argued, involve the rejection of the idea of a 'profit', but it lays a claim to it and its disposal in reinvestment or social expenditure on behalf of those who create it—the workers both by hand and brain.

Thus the definition of a worker is extended to include all wage and salary earners and paves the way for the extension of trade unionism into the realms of clerical white collar, scientific and technical and managerial work which is now gaining pace in Britain.

The phrase 'common ownership' is cast widely enough to embrace all forms of enterprise, including nationalised industries, municipal and co-operative enterprises, which it is envisaged should provide the basis for the control and operation of manufacturing, distribution and the banks and insurance companies.

In practice, Labour programmes and manifestos over the years have focused primarily on the great monopolies of financial, economic and industrial power which have grown out of the theoretical operation of a free market economy. For the ideas of *laissez-faire* and free enterprise propounded by Adam Smith and carried forward by the Manchester School of Liberal Economists until they reappeared under the new guise of monetarism, have never achieved what was claimed for them.

Today, capitalist monopolies in Britain and throughout the world have long since 'repealed the laws of supply and demand' and have become centres of political power concerned principally with safeguarding the financial investors who have lost the benefits of shareholder democracy and the great self-perpetuating hierarchy of managers who run them. For this purpose they control the media, engage in direct propaganda and on occasions have been found guilty of corrupt practices on a massive scale or have intervened directly to support governments that will allow them to continue their exploitation of men and raw materials for their own benefit.

There is one other phrase in paragraph four which is less well known. This is the commitment to 'the best obtainable system of popular administration and control of each industry or service'. It is from this phrase that we can draw our authority for the present pressure for industrial democracy, workers' control, or self-management, which is clearly the next step we must take if the existing public sector is not to develop into a corporatist nightmare permitting the worst forms of managerial authoritarianism to creep back through the back door in the public service, public agencies and publicly owned industries.

The ideas of workers' control have roots going deep into the history of our movement, and at one stage syndicalism, based on industrial unionism, was seen as a substitute for, and as an alternative to, parliamentary democracy. Since then there has been a great deal of rethinking about the meaning of industrial democracy in the Labour Movement. It is clear that a move in that direction would substantially alter the role of the trade unions; since it must involve the acceptance by the unions of a far greater degree of responsibility. Though few Socialists would deny that this responsibility must necessarily pass to those who work, there are great dangers in involving the unions in responsibility if the necessary powers do not go with it.

Whatever problems may lie ahead, no one in the movement doubts that progress must be made, first to bring labour into a truly equal partnership in controlling industry and then in reorganising, so that those who actively create the wealth can shape the processes by which it is done and determine (within the framework of law and the needs of the nation) how the surpluses should be applied to develop our manufacturing, productive and service industries. Investors there will always be, but there is no valid reason why the investors' money should give them first claim to control, before those who invest their lives. Political democracy wrested the control of Parliament from those who owned the lands and the factories. Industrial democracy is a logical and necessary development of it.

Paragraph Five merits a special mention because of the general language in which it is couched. It commits the party to work for 'the political, social and economic emancipation of the people' extending our interest beyond those who are actually at work to the old, the young, the sick and, indeed, to the whole community. It is often wrongly argued that Labour is only concerned with active, working trade unionists, to the exclusion of everyone else. Yet even the most cursory glance at the immense range of interests that characterises the work of the party and the unions will show how false that charge really is.

It is true that our formal links are with the organised Labour Movement, but that movement has always concerned itself with the interests of the nation and its people. Labour sees itself as their guardian, which, through its unity alone, can mount the strength to be an effective champion for their interests against the immensely rich, powerful and influential forces that constitute modern capitalism.

Paragraphs Six and Seven represent the British Labour Movement's internationalist stance in association with the peoples of the world and the expression of that role is to be found in the work of the Socialist International, the international trade union movement, and the great help and assistance that the British unions and the party give to those who are struggling to achieve in their countries the same objectives as we have set ourselves here.

I have commented at length on Clause IV, both because it is a remarkable summary of the experience that went before, and because of its growing relevance today as capitalism moves into decline.[21] It must, for these reasons, remain at the core of our work.

The Labour Movement

The history of the Labour Movement cannot only be seen as the story of Christian philosophers or, for that matter, trade union leaders and Labour parliamentarians. For ideas without action will for ever remain as academic works, scholarly but sterile, and leaders are only important in so far as they truly represent those whom they serve. The real history of any popular movement is made by those, almost always anonymous, who throughout history have fought for what they believe in, organised others to join them, and have done so against immense odds and with nothing to gain for themselves, learning from their experience and leaving others to distil that experience and to use it again to advance the cause.

British socialism, then, is an amalgam of that experience, a blend of theory and practice built up out of many centuries of effort and thought; drawing its inspiration from many sources and absorbing them all into a belief in basic human equality and freedom, to be expressed in the democratic forms of chapel, union and Parliament, to which all power should be accountable. The main instrument for advancing these ideas since the nineteenth century has been, and remains, the organised Labour Movement. That is why it is so powerful and so humane and so relevant today.

ISSUES OF THE
1970s

2

Labour's Industrial Programme

Like most Labour governments, the one elected in February 1974 came to power with a plan for restoring the economy. The plan had been spelled out in some detail in the party programme published before the annual conference six months earlier. This had committed the party to 'a fundamental and irreversible shift of the balance of power and wealth in favour of working people and their families'.[1] The phrase was repeated in the general election manifestos the following February and October, which were generally believed to be the most radical since 1945.

The core of Labour's programme was an industrial strategy designed to restore industrial investment and so construct a sound base for the party's social aspirations. The principal instruments of the strategy were to be (a) a system of planning agreements, under which leading companies would be obliged to disclose their investment and other plans to the government and their workers; (b) a state holding company, the National Enterprise Board (NEB), with power to extend public ownership into profit-making sectors of the economy. The February manifesto also added: 'Whenever we give direct aid to a company out of public funds we shall in return reserve the right to take a share of the ownership of the company.'[2] The October manifesto repeated and elaborated on all these proposals. It also contained a promise to introduce legislation which would 'help forward our plans for a radical extension of industrial democracy in both the private and public sectors'.[3]

Although it was later to become controversial the Labour programme, at the time it was originally proposed, enjoyed the support of all sections of the party. This, for example, is what Harold Wilson told the 1973 annual conference on the question of future government aid to private industry:[4]

> In politics the reach of public responsibility and public money should never exceed the grasp of public control. But it means that in economic and industrial policy, from now on, the grasp of national control must extend as far as the reach of government aid.

This was Harold Wilson on planning agreements:

> The Planning Agreements system will be reinforced by a new Industry Act. This Act will provide the Government with powers, powers which it will use ... to seek agreement with companies over a wide range of industrial matters, including prices, profits, investment programmes, overseas trade, industrial relations and industrial democracy, and if necessary in the national interest, to issue directives on any of these subjects.

And this was Harold Wilson on the National Enterprise Board:

> ... I must once again emphasise that the role of the National Enterprise Board is not just confined to the duties of a public holding and management agency ... It will act also as a means to a further substantial expansion of public ownership through its power to take a controlling interest in relevant companies in profitable manufacturing industries.

When Labour were returned to government in 1974 I was appointed by Harold Wilson as Secretary of State for Industry. The job of giving practical expression to these election promises therefore fell to me. What follows is a record of how we at the Department of Industry set about the task. Before that, however, let me try and make the case for fundamental changes to the way our economy is organised.

The Case for Change

The Labour Party exists to bring about a shift in the balance of power and wealth. As a Labour Party, born out of the trade union movement, we represent—politically—the same people whom the unions represent industrially. We also aim to make economic power more fully accountable to the community, to workers and the consumer. We aim to eliminate poverty, to achieve a far greater economic equality and meet urgent social needs. This is not a new challenge, but a very old one. As more people become dissatisfied with the obvious inequality that exists in Britain and the growing abuse of business power, the demand for fundamental reform will grow too. Unless it is met, the consent necessary to run our society will not be available.

The 1970s provided us with many examples of the abuse of financial power. There were individual scandals such as the one involving Lonrho which the Conservative Prime Minister, Mr Heath, described as the 'unacceptable face of capitalism'.[5] Firms may be able to get away with the payment of £38,000 a year to part-time chairmen if no one else knows about it. But when it becomes public and we know that the chairman, as a Conservative M.P., supports a statutory wages policy to keep down the wage of low-paid workers, some earning less than £20 a week at that time, it becomes intolerable. There was the case of the drug company, Hoffman-La Roche, who were grossly overcharging the National Health Service.[6] There was also the initial refusal by Distillers to compensate the thalidomide children properly.

There were other broader scandals such as those involving speculation in property and agricultural land; the whole industry of tax avoidance; the casino-like atmosphere of the Stock Exchange. Millions of people who experience real problems in Britain are gradually learning about all this on radio and television and from the press. Such things are a cynical affront to the struggle that ordinary people have to feed and clothe their families.

But the problem goes deeper than that. Workers have no legal rights to be consulted when the firms for which they work are taken over. They are sold off like cattle when a firm changes hands with no guarantee for the future. The rapid growth of trade union membership among white-collar workers and even managers indicates the strength of feelings about that. Not just the economic but also the political power of big business, especially the multinationals, has come into the open.

In Chile, the ITT plotted to overthrow an elected President. The American arms companies, Lockheed and Northrop, have been shown to have civil servants, generals, ministers and even prime ministers, in democratic countries as well as dictatorships, on their payroll. The Watergate revelations have shown how big business funds were used in an attempt to corrupt the American democratic process. In Britain we have had massive political campaigns also financed by big business to oppose the Labour Party's programme for public ownership and to secure the re-election of Conservative governments. Big business also underwrote the cost of the campaign to keep Britain in the Common Market at the time of the 1975 referendum.

Leaving aside the question of abuse, the sheer concentration of industrial and economic power is now a major political factor. The spate of mergers in recent years in Britain alone — and their expected continuation — can be expressed like this: in 1950 the top 100 companies in Britain produced about 20 per cent of our national output. By 1973 they produced 46 per cent. And at this rate, by 1980, they will produce 66 per cent — two-thirds of our national output.[7] Many of them will be operating multinationally, exporting capital and jobs and siphoning off profits to where the taxes are most favourable.

The banks, insurance companies and financial institutions are also immensely powerful. In June 1973 I was invited to speak at a conference organised by the *Financial Times* and the *Investors Chronicle*. It was held in the London Hilton, and before going I added up the value of the total assets of the banks and other financial institutions represented in the audience. They were worth at that time about £95,000 million. This was at the time about twice as much as the Gross National Product of the United Kingdom and four or five times the total sum raised in taxation by the British Government each year.

The Labour Party must ask what effect all this power will have on the nature of our democracy. Britain is proud of its system of parliamentary democracy, its local democracy and its free trade unions. But rising against this we have the growing power of the Common Market which will strip our elected House of Commons of its control over some key economic decisions. This has greatly weakened British democracy at a time when economic power is growing stronger.

I have spelled this out because it is the background against which our policy proposals have been developed. In the light of our experience in earlier governments we believed it would be necessary for government to have far greater powers over industry. These are some of the measures we were aiming at in the Industry Bill presented to Parliament in 1975, shortly after our return to power:

The right to require disclosure of information by companies.

The right of government to invest in private companies requiring support.

The provision for joint planning between government and firms.

The right to acquire firms, with the approval of Parliament.

The right to protect firms from foreign takeovers.

The extension of the present insurance companies' provisions for ministerial control over board members.

The extension of the idea of Receivership to cover the defence of the interests of workers and the nation.

Safeguards against the abuse of power by global companies.

If we are to have a managed economy—and that seems to be accepted—the question is: 'In whose interests is it to be managed?' We intend to manage it in the interests of working people and their families. But we do not accept the present corporate structure of Government Boards, Commissions and Agents, working secretly and not accountable to Parliament. The powers we want must be subjected to House of Commons approval when they are exercised.

On the question of public ownership. When we had been in government in the past we tried to work by the indirect method of using a system of negative controls and huge public subsidies to try and inject the national interest into boardroom thinking. It was a great improvement on the old-fashioned doctrine of *laissez-faire*, but our experience and that of Mr

Heath's 1970–74 government has convinced us that policies based on carrot and stick are not adequate. Public ownership is necessary to meet the needs of the people of this country as they turn to others for protection from the abuse of business power to which they are now exposed. Those who talk about public ownership as if it in some way represented a threat had better realise the truth which is that there are millions of workers, and I mean workers right up to management level, who have been much more frightened of the possibility that Slater Walker will take them over and sell their assets and close them down than of anything we may do. Moreover, the violence of the attacks upon our public ownership plans and on us for defending them launched by big business and by the media confirm our judgment that these plans are a serious threat, as they are intended to be, to the unaccountable power they wield and the unacceptable privileges they defend with that power. We should all now have learned the hard way that you cannot bully and bribe businessmen into pursuing policies to meet our regional employment needs, our investment needs and our national interests, against the interests of their shareholders. We have come to the end of that road.

The plain truth is that Britain has suffered a relative industrial decline over a long time under the governments of both parties. Let us take, for example, the average annual growth of manufacturing output from 1953 to 1975 (see Table 1).[8]

Table 1

	%
United Kingdom	2·6
France	5·5
Italy	7·4
Germany	6·3
Japan	11·6

Next, let's take the average annual growth of manufactured exports by volume in the period 1954 to 1977 (see Table 2).[9]

Table 2

	%
United Kingdom	6·6
France	13·6
West Germany	14·5
Italy	21·4
Japan	23·1

Finally, if we take the investment per employee in manu-facturing—that is the amount of horsepower, machinery and equipment behind the average British worker—we find that in 1974 there was $920-worth of investment behind the average worker in the United Kingdom, while in France the figure was $2,288, in Germany $1,707, in Italy $1,469 and in Japan $2,141.[10]

If we look at the basic statistics and figures over a long period, we find that a mixed economy, in the way in which it has been operating, has not brought to the people of this country the results which they might otherwise have had. This is why we are now discussing the needs for an extension of public owner-ship to some of the sector leaders in successful manufacturing industry; well beyond the basic industries or those that have obviously failed—like shipbuilding—which have been the only candidates for public ownership in the past. We are not interested in ownership just for the sake of ownership. We are concerned with the power that ownership carries with it to shape our future.

What is at issue is not the precise number of firms which we might need during the next Parliaments—although it might be noted in passing that if Slater Walker can acquire twenty-nine companies in a single year—1972—a government target of twenty-five over a far longer period does not sound excessive.

It is not the number, but the principle, of really substantial extensions of public ownership into manufacturing that does matter. Put this way, as it should be, the case is very powerful indeed.

Whatever the merits of these arguments may be, some people assumed automatically that if the Labour Party put them forward at a general election we would be heavily defeated. In 1974 we did put them forward and we won — twice.

We have to ask ourselves, do the British people really want a society in which industrialists and bankers have more power over Britain's economic future than the governments they elect? Can we ignore the fact that many workers — right up to management level — are also now more worried about takeover bids and asset stripping? Maybe if the choice was between a concentration of power in public hands or tens of thousands of small, intimately competing small businesses, the voter would think there was safety in numbers. But that is not the choice. The choice is between a growing concentration of private power held in a very few — closely linked — hands, not accountable to the community. Or greater accountability to workers, consumers and to the people — from within the public sector.

Opening the Books

After Labour were returned in February 1974 one of the first things we did at the Department of Industry was to try and see that more information was made available to Parliament and the public about the issues with which we would have to deal. One example of this policy was the publication of the amounts of public money that had gone into leading companies in all forms of grants and subsidies over the previous few years. There seemed to me no reason why the details of tax-payers' money paid by the Government to industrial firms should be confidential. Spokesmen for industry have always argued that we in Britain have a flourishing free enterprise system operating independently of government and upon whose profits and the wages they pay our present and future prospects depend, and that this system must be maintained. But the plain truth is that over many years, and under all governments, large sums of tax-payers' money have been paid to privately owned companies in our effort to strengthen them and provide more jobs. When we took office in 1974 there were no fewer than sixteen separate financial assistance schemes in existence. These included regional development, investment support, general assistance, aerospace, shipbuilding, tourism and research and development. On coming into office we found that in the four years up to March 1974 over £3 billion had been paid by government under these subsidy programmes. We decided to publish these figures, together with details of the main recipients. These are repeated in Table 3 (in an updated form).

Table 3[11]

Years	Government aid £m
1970/1	819·4
1971/2	711·1
1972/3	603·7
1973/4	690·3
1974/5	776·4
1975/6	1,167·6
1976/7	928·5

In publishing these figures, it is not suggested that the purposes for which the money is provided are wrong, nor even hinted that the amount should be cut, nor are we blaming past governments for paying the money, or criticising the industrialists who took it. We are saying that these figures throw new light on the argument that private enterprise, free from public support, exists in Britain in the form in which we are told it exists. We are also saying that the national purposes for which these policies were developed have not been achieved. After all this expenditure, Britain still has inadequate investment in modern plant and equipment, serious regional employment problems and a poor record of economic growth. This then should be the starting point for public discussions about Labour's industrial policy.

Planning Agreements and the NEB

The main instruments of our industrial policy were planning agreements and the National Enterprise Board which were provided for in the Industry Bill introduced into Parliament in 1975. That same year we introduced legislation to take the aircraft and shipbuilding industries, both of which were already subsidised massively out of public funds, into public ownership. In order that these policies should be developed in co-operation with the trade union movement, a trade union adviser was appointed by the Department of Industry. His job was to supervise consultation with the leaders of all the major trade unions whose members work in the industries affected by our new policies.

Planning agreements were designed to secure the co-operation of leading companies with national economic priorities, in return for government support to industry such as financial aid and orders from government departments or nationalised industries. The basis for such agreements was to include such criteria as price control, the level of home and overseas sales, the regional distribution of employment, domestic investment levels, industrial relations practices and product development. These agreements were to be on a tripartite basis with the unions involved from the outset. Once corporate policies in these areas had been agreed on an annual and a rolled forward five-year basis, the government would be in a position to grant selective financial assistance for at least the minimum period necessary to meet the demands of medium-term corporate planning.

The idea was that financial aid to major companies should be linked to the objectives of the planning agreements. The information drawn from them would then be available to the government in planning its own strategy. The firms to be included in this system were initially intended to number about one hundred, controlling about half our manufacturing output. Since the great majority of these hundred or so firms have overseas subsidiaries or are themselves part of wider international groupings, this new conditional system of aid, combining both incentives and sanctions, would form an important instrument for securing the compliance of large multi-national corporations with the government's own economic objectives.[12]

The National Enterprise Board was designed to be set alongside the planning agreements system for the purpose of securing those objectives which can only be achieved by direct public intervention. The NEB was to be formed initially out of existing government holdings in industry such as BP, Rolls-Royce and Short Brothers, with a substantial addition of companies from the private sector. The idea was that the NEB should invest in potentially the most profitable areas of industry and should in the long term make profits which could be reinvested so that eventually it could extend its influence over a very substantial area of the economy. Obviously, to achieve this purpose the NEB would have to have enormous funds at its disposal. In February 1975, during the Second Reading of the Industry Bill which gave birth to both planning agreements and the NEB, it was decided that the NEB would have an initial budget of £700 millions, with power, if Parliament approved, to increase this to £1,000 millions. This was in addition to provisions already made under the Conservatives' 1972 Industry Act for public intervention in Industry.[13]

Public Ownership

Planning agreements, the National Enterprise Board and many other aspects of Labour's industrial strategy involve, as we have seen, a considerable extension of public ownership. By 1977 the public sector employed 7·38 million workers and accounted for about 29·7 per cent of Britain's gross national product.[14] This being so, we should constantly have under review the aims and objectives of public ownership and remain constantly on the look-out for ways in which it can be improved and adapted to remain in line with the aspirations of the Labour Movement.

The idea of government intervention in private industry is not the prerogative of the Left alone. There are many on the Right who have accepted intervention if it is necessary to prop up this system in which they believe. For example, Winston Churchill in 1914 moved the Second Reading of a Bill enabling the Liberal Government, of which he was then a member, to acquire a majority holding in the old Anglo-Persian Oil Company (now British Petroleum). He had this to say about the concession which the company had received with government blessing:

It would enormously strengthen the Company and increase the value of their property. If this consequence arose from the necessary action of the State, why should not the State share in the advantage which we created? If, in any case, we had to go so far, why should we not go a step further? Was it not wiser, was it not more profitable on every ground, naval, financial and indeed equitable, to acquire control of an enterprise which we are bound to help and bound to enrich and on which, to a large extent, we must rely?[15]

The Conservative Party, during its various periods of government, has also endorsed the idea that certain monopolies should be in public hands. The formation of the BBC, of the original Electricity Board, the public ownership of Imperial Airways (the forerunner of British Airways), and Rolls-Royce in 1971 are all examples of industries taken into public ownership by Tory governments. The Tories have long accepted, where basic industries *have* to be sustained and cannot be profitable, that public ownership is an appropriate remedy. If, as a result of that, private industry can be further subsidised by causing the publicly owned basic industries to supply their goods below cost to the private sector that is all right too. All this is worth recalling, even if only as a reminder that actions of nationalisation do not inevitably follow from socialist motives, nor lead to socialised industries. Indeed, these examples act as a warning against believing that nationalisation, of itself, represents an automatic road to a more democratic or responsible control of industry.

The record of the nationalised industries is something of which the Labour Movement can be justly proud. Certainly the investment necessary to carry through re-equipment and expansion did not take place and the contribution made to public output by the public sector has revealed an efficiency in management at least as great as that to be found in the private sector. But the time has come to reassess the role of the public corporation and public ownership.

We must recognise that the nationalisation of our basic industries, in the form in which it was carried out, has been a disappointment to many who saw in public ownership something that would transform the role of the workers in the industries concerned. The aspirations of workers advocating public ownership is set out in a very moving passage which I would like to quote, from the evidence given to the Sankey Commission set up in 1919 to consider the future of the mining industry. Mr William Straker, the Secretary of the Northumberland Miners' Association, in submitting his evidence to that Commission, began with the following words:[16]

In deciding what is to be the character of mines administration it is necessary to remember that workmen are more than machines, or even 'hands' as they are so often termed. Industrial unrest is a question about which everyone is concerned, yet there is a general lack of appreciation of what is the real root of this unrest. In the past workmen have thought that if they could secure higher wages and better conditions they would be content. Employers have thought that if they granted these things the workers ought to be content. Wages and conditions have been improved — but the discontent and the unrest have not disappeared, and many good people have come to the conclusion that working men are so unreasonable that it is useless trying to satisfy them. The fact is that the unrest is deeper than can be reached by merely pounds, shillings and pence, necessary as they were. The root of the matter is the straining of the spirit of man to be free. Once he secures the freedom of the spirit he will, as a natural sequence, secure a material welfare equal to what the united brains and hand can wring from mother earth and her surrounding atmosphere. Any administration of the mines under nationalisation must not leave the mineworker in the position of a mere wage-earner, whose sole energies are directed by the will of another. He must have a share in the management of the industry in which he is engaged, and understand all about the purpose and destination of the product he is producing; he must know both the productive and commercial side of the industry. He must feel that the industry is being run by him in order to produce coal for the use of the community, instead of profit for the few people. He would thus feel the responsibility that would rest on him as a citizen, and direct his energies for the common good. This ideal cannot be reached all at once owing to the way in which private ownership had deliberately kept the worker in ignorance regarding the industry; but as that knowledge, which has been denied him, grows, as it will do under nationalisation, he will take his rightful place as a man. Only then will labour unrest, which is the present hope of the world, disappear. The mere granting of the 30 per cent and the shorter hours demanded will not prevent unrest, neither will nationalisation with bureaucratic administration. Just as we are making political democracy world-wide, so we must have industrial democracy, in order that men may be free.

That is a very remarkable statement, from a working miner, of the aspirations which led so many of his fellow workers to press for public ownership, raising hopes which have not been realised by the structure of nationalisation which we have adopted.

The *first* and central problem of nationalisation must now be seen as hinging on the extent to which we can develop real industrial democracy within those industries. We have waited too long for the transformation of the public corporation. Workers' self-management, when it comes, should come from the working membership of the trade unions, from those with direct experience in the industries. We must reject the idea that one worker on the board is industrial democracy. We must reject co-ownership. We must reject phoney works councils not rooted in the strength and structure and traditions of the trade union movement. All these are window dressing designed to divert the demand for democratic control into utterly harmless challenge. We should be talking about the transfer of power within industry and we should not accept existing patterns of nationalisation as a form for the future. We have had enough experience now to know that nationalisation plus Lord Robens does not add up to socialism.

The *second* question that we need to look at again is the relationship between the public sector and the consumers of their product. In the case of some nationalised industries, as for example coal or electricity, the consumers fall into two groups: industrial consumers who are looking for the cheapest and most reliable source of fuel to maintain their competitive position, and domestic consumers who may not be able to pay the high cost of energy bills. Big monopolies must have special provision made to see that they do not abuse their powers. Profit cannot be the only criterion. Consumer representation should be made more effective in shaping the decisions of public industries.

Third, the nationalised industries must find new ways of relating to the communities in which their operations are conducted. Some form of local accountability for local or national decisions by the nationalised industries should be provided to allow the local authorities, representing the areas in which the industries operate, to be heard before decisions are made.

It is interesting to note that whereas Herbert Morrison,[17] the architect of much of Labour's early nationalisation programme, played such a notable part in joining together the fragmented activities of various independent transport and electricity undertakings, we should now be considering how that power can be made accountable to the very communities away from which it was initially taken. But there is no doubt whatsoever that, for example in the case of the closures in the steel and mining industries, or the phasing out of old power stations, provision for proper local consultation must be made.

Fourth, there must also be provision for nationalised industries themselves to take much fuller account of the supply industries which depend on them for orders. It is very well known, for example, that the Post Office, in determining its own domestic exchange equipment in the late 1950s and early 1960s, took too little account of the small export market for the electronic exchanges that it preferred to the semi-automatic cross-bar system which was being used world-wide. As a result, the British telecommunications industry was denied the domestic orders it needed as a foundation for a successful export effort. Similarly, the Central Electricity Generating Board, by insisting upon maintenance of competing companies, failed to provide the basis for the replication of designs which would have been necessary for those industries to sell British nuclear power stations abroad. The supplying industries' interests in the orderly development of investment programmes should be much clearer in focus and considered in each case before investment programmes are approved.

Fifth, and most importantly in the context of energy and transport, ways have got to be found of providing for an integration of the planning mechanisms of nationalised industries that interrelate with one another. The trade union movement has long demanded the development of an integrated national energy and transport policy. It is interesting that Herbert Morrison himself thought in terms of a National Transport Corporation. Indeed the post-war Transport Commission was set up with a view to achieving just that. Similarly, the TUC had, until recently, been demanding a National Fuel Corporation to bring about the integration of the various energy industries for the common good. However, the price that would have to be paid for a solution of that kind would be so great in terms of size, centralisation and bureaucracy that we must now question if this is the right solution.

My own experience in dealing with nationalised industries from my time as Postmaster-General in 1964 and later as Minister of Technology, Minister of Power, Secretary for Industry and Secretary for Energy has absolutely convinced me that the role of co-ordination is essentially a political, economic and industrial policy role which cannot and must not be separated from the democratic responsibilities of ministers answerable to Parliament. The government should take responsibility for integrating the industrial policies of publicly owned industries, where they overlap. This responsibility should be embodied in statute.

Sixth, this brings me to the central question of the relations that ought to exist between the government and the nationalised industries. Although Herbert Morrison tried very hard indeed to establish the framework for that relationship it is manifestly clear that it has not been a satisfactory one. There is too much secrecy surrounding that relationship and the appointments made by ministers to boards involve an unacceptable level of unaccountable patronage.

In the absence of real statutory powers, there has developed a tradition of back-door interference which is both frustrating for ministers and irritating for the boards of corporations because the whole basis of the relationship has been left too vague to be effective. The importance of getting relations between government and the nationalised industries right is so crucial that it may well be necessary to develop new institutions which, for example, might allow civil servants to serve on the boards of nationalised industries and to give the minister an effective power of specific directive which is now denied in all cases except the National Enterprise Board and the British National Oil Corporation. Relations with the government should be put on a sounder and more open footing, so that proper accountability can take place.

Seventh, we must look again at the relationship between the nationalised industries and Parliament. The tradition of non-accountability to the House of Commons as a whole, combined with the provision of special enquiries by the nationalised industries' Select Committee, represents an uneasy balance between detailed interrogation and a general disclaimer on the part of ministers for the conduct of the industries for which they have overall responsibility.

Eighth, we must look, in the context of our experience with the existing nationalised industries, at the way in which public ownership and control should be extended into new sectors of industry—notably profitable manufacturing industry, which in the 1974 manifesto we committed ourselves to undertake as an act of policy. As we have seen, the National Enterprise Board is intended to acquire individual firms rather than whole industries and this development has still to be shaped within the context of real public accountability.

We must also look again at the role of municipal socialism and here the relevance of General Powers Provisions for local authorities is of growing importance. This would involve giving local authorities greater powers to aid and take a stake in private industry within their areas. Some authorities such as Salford and Wandsworth have already taken initiatives for stimulating local industry.[18]

All these problems need to be tackled as part of the development of industrial democracy within the public sector, present and future. We must also argue out new objectives for the nationalised industries, and then invite those who work within them to undertake the task of seeing how they can best be implemented within the industries in which they work. We should surely have had enough of purely external enquiries, either written by outsiders with no knowledge of the industry, or, worse still, by consultants who are brought in to do a quick report and then disappear with no responsibility for implementation.

Herbert Morrison's achievement in establishing our main public industries was a formidable one and history will record it as such. But it is now equally important that the Labour Movement should turn its mind to the transformation of those public corporations into expressions of our socialist purpose. Namely, that policies and institutions must serve the people and not become the masters.

Industrial Democracy

In the long discussion about industrial democracy various proposals have been put forward by management and others which, whatever their merits, do not effectively extend democratic controls. These have included profit-sharing or co-partnership under which workers hold a few shares in the companies in which they work. This does not resolve the basic conflict of interest that exists in industry, does not give the worker-shareholders any real share of power in the firm, and could put their savings and their pensions — as well as their jobs — at risk, if the firm collapses.

Then there was the idea of the single worker on the board. This proposal, adopted in some nationalised industries, has not enlarged the power of the workforce since most worker directors have not been elected by, nor are they accountable to, the workforce as a whole.

There have also been elected works councils. Separated from the organised trade union movement these can only weaken the movement without providing a representative system of comparable strength.

Finally, the most enlightened management is now waking up

to the need for new approaches, such as programmes of job enrichment and better company communications. However successful these may be in themselves, none of these proposals constitutes any shift towards democratic control.

In recent years the demand from workers for greater industrial democracy has also manifested itself in a number of different ways. These have included the 1971 work-in at Upper Clyde Shipbuilders; the battles to establish worker co-operatives at Triumph of Meriden, at Fisher Bendix in Kirkby and at the *Scottish Daily News*; proposals by the shop stewards at the British Aircraft Corporation in Bristol for workers' control of the aircraft industry; and the growth of combine committees bringing together shop stewards from different plants in a single firm, or different firms in a whole industry. The Lucas Aerospace Combine is perhaps the best known of these. Eighteen months as Secretary of State for Industry allowed me to assist workers engaged in each of these different forms of struggle.

The Upper Clyde Work-in

My first experience of dealing with Upper Clyde Shipbuilders was as Minister of Technology in the 1966–70 Labour Government, during the period before the Tories decided it should go bankrupt.[19] And if you want an example of the old type of state intervention, masterminded from the top, you could not have a better one than the Geddes Report[20] and its implementation by the Shipbuilding Industry Board, which was my responsibility before 1970. The policy ran like this: the accumulation of a number of sick shipyards into a single privately owned shipbuilding firm; the injection into it of technocratic management, much of it from outside the industry; and of course the rejection not only of public ownership but also of the idea that in the solution of the problems of the shipbuilding industry those who actually worked in the industry had any contribution to make. If I was educated by my experience, which is what I have tried to be, I was educated by the experience of trying it another way.

The first great example of change in the thinking of the

Labour Party on this question was undoubtedly the work-in at UCS. The UCS decided to work in when the Tory Industry Minister, John Davies, told them they were ready to go into bankruptcy and collapse. Mr Heath imagined that the work-in was a little local difficulty that would quickly be forgotten. Trouble in the Clyde after all was not unfamiliar to Tory governments. The 'Red Clydesiders', he thought, could be easily contained. But in fact the Upper Clyde Shipbuilders gave vitality to the concept of industrial democracy in a manner we had not seen for many years. I am not saying that the UCS sit-in was about industrial democracy. As became clear, it was about the right to work. But the fact that such a campaign was linked to a demand to be allowed to continue to work, coming not from the top, but from the people in the yards: that was a very important development. I haven't forgotten the impact that it had even in the parliamentary Labour Party. As a result the parliamentary Labour Party adopted ahead of the party conference — and that's saying something — a resolution to bring public ownership to the shipbuilding industry, which was a complete reversal of Labour Government policy in 1964–70.

During our period of opposition this was absorbed into the manifesto so that it became absolutely clear that an incoming Labour Government could not, and should not, think of its industrial policy simply in terms of what a Labour minister might do in his office, but rather in terms of a partnership between the trade union movement and the Labour Government. That was the first step beyond the corporatist idea of public ownership planned from the top. This must be attributed entirely to what was being done on the shop floor during that period, and if those events had not occurred when they did and in the form they did, the Labour manifesto of 1974 would not have reflected any aspirations beyond the traditional Morrisonian approach to public ownership.

The Workers' Co-ops [21]

When in the spring of 1974 we came to power we found that some of the other campaigns that had inspired us — at Meriden and at Fisher Bendix — were still in progress. As everyone knows, it is possible to say one thing in opposition and another thing in government. The first question we had to ask ourselves was what should be the attitude of Labour ministers to pressures brought from within the Labour Movement, as distinct from what should be said by a Labour ex-minister or shadow minister speaking from the security of opposition?

It was out of the determination to maintain the government-trade union partnership that we began the first experiments in workers' co-operatives: Meriden, Kirkby Manufacturing and Engineering, and the *Scottish Daily News*. They pose important questions.

First of all, why were these three experiments chosen as distinct from a whole host of others, why were these the ones where something happened? Let's be quite clear, it was not because of the Secretary of State for Industry. It had nothing whatever to do with me. It was because in cases of this kind, as at UCS, the experiments selected themselves. A body of men and women on the shop floor were prepared to go through the agony (and it was agony) of struggle for work, so that out of their struggle could be bred a capacity to cope with the responsibility brought by success.

For example, by the time they won, Meriden had been battling away for eighteen months.[22] I visited them on many occasions, at times when I didn't know whether we would succeed or fail. I drove in at 2 o'clock one Sunday morning on my way back from Bristol. They were still at work in the shed there, using a temporary lighting system because the firm's owners, Norton Villiers Triumph, had switched off the lights. There they were. They didn't know I was coming. I went past the brazier at 2 a.m. and in the shed they were busy designing the left-hand gear shift. The spirit at Meriden sustained them and carried them forward.

The same was true at Kirkby.[23] At first there was suspicion among shop stewards when they came to the Department of Industry, suspicion about what we were trying to say to them. First of all they said: 'We want you to save the firm. That's what we want. Will you give money to save the firm?' We had to get them to believe that we were really not interested in saving the firm but we were interested in saving jobs and saving production. It took a very long time to persuade them that it was not a con-trick by a minister who was finding some excuse for not helping them in the ordinary way that ministers help firms — by giving money to the firm. The firm went bust, but the Kirkby Co-operative generated the will and the machinery to carry the work through. The co-operative lasted about four years, but finally had to close in April 1979 after the government refused to lend it any more money.

The third co-operative was the *Scottish Daily News* which enjoyed a short and troubled life in 1974, arising from the ashes of the *Scottish Daily Express* which had been closed with the loss of nearly 2,000 jobs. A government loan of £1.2 million proved insufficient to help the co-op survive and it collapsed after publishing for only six months.

The Lessons of the Workers' Co-ops

These Co-operatives have shown a number of very important things. First of all they have shown the importance of self-selection. When people say to me, for example, 'Why didn't you set up a co-operative when Aston Martin went bust?' I have to reply that in Newport Pagnell, where Aston Martin was based, male unemployment was 1·8 per cent and quite frankly the workers at Aston Martin didn't want a workers' co-operative and there was nothing that I could have done to get a co-operative going if that was not what they actually wanted. Where changes were made, the impetus, the energy, the organisational ability, was coming from the shop floor.

Unless a Labour Government can find some way of discovering and encouraging, harnessing and working with this sort of feeling, it is inevitably going to be driven back on to a plan for industry thought out at the top and imposed from the top which, however well organised and well intentioned, in many respects will not be so far from what might be done by others such as the Tories, whose concept of intervention, or even of public ownership, ought to be very different from our own.

So now we need to study the experience of those three co-operatives, and study it in detail with those involved so that we may learn something from it. People say to me: 'What a tragedy that the idea of a co-operative should be launched always in such unfavourable circumstances.' Of course that was the whole point. Because, until the circumstances were unfavourable, this energy and drive and organisation never emerged. There wasn't machinery in government (and there still isn't today) to make it possible for people whose prospects seem better than these three to be assisted.

This brings us to the second question: what can government do when the desire is there, but the skill is lacking and without the skill the will is weak? I began—again a very modest contribution—the idea of putting consultants to work for the workforce instead of only for the government or the management. And I had some interesting discussions with consultants to whom it had never occurred that their tasks would be to write a report to show the workforce how to keep their jobs instead of showing the management how to get rid of these jobs.

Shop stewards would often say to me: 'Look, we would like to do this, but we don't read a balance sheet and we don't know how.' This raises two questions. First of all I had to be very candid and say: 'I am not a qualified accountant. I can't, without assistance, make sense of complicated economic and industrial problems brought to me as a minister. Now why am I different? Because, as Secretary of State for Industry, all these people are laid on to do it for me and it is a skill that you can hire, like any other skill, such as that of a doctor, a dentist or a lawyer, and what matters is that you should hire in the interests of the objectives you have in mind.' So we made consultants available to people in those situations. There were other cases too.

There is no reason whatever why government—a Labour Government—if it bends its mind to the problem arising in such cases, cannot cut short the long process of learning industrial management by providing skill on contract to those who are confronted with these problems.

Further, this new experience points to the crucial problem of whether we can't raise the level of understanding of these complicated yet mechanical types of knowledge and skill which people need in these circumstances. I am very glad to see that the trade union movement is now beginning to make its own demands for access to funds for training on a larger scale, because, like any skill, if you get people of the high degree of intelligence who are to be found in industry among the shop stewards' committees, it is really not too complicated for them to lift the level of their abilities with a little bit of help. Labour ministers have to try it all the time—we are not all very successful, but it is not beyond our capacity to learn.

Democracy in the Public Sector

At this point I should say something about the *steel industry*. In this case, and this highlights the difference I tried to establish earlier, you are dealing with an industry already nationalised, so the great argument about public ownership is settled. But of course when the British Steel Corporation produced its development plan there was no real consultation with those who were concerned in working a nationalised industry. But, because the public ownership issue was out of the way, one focused to the heart of the question, which is that of instituting the democratic control of an industry already in public ownership. And although we began in a modest way (and I don't want to make great claims), we had the review of the steel development plan. We also worked with the Action Committees at Shotton and Shelton and elsewhere to review the plan, and see what its implications were and how we could overcome the acute problems of redundancy that flowed from it.[24]

This is worth studying too, because in the end I had one or two disagreements with Sir Montague Finniston[25] which I won't go into in any detail, except to say that the disagreements were not about whether I wanted to run the steel industry (which I am wholly ill-equipped to do) but about whether it was right that the steel industry should be run by a public corporation without consultation with the people who work in it. That was what the issue was, and that is still a crucial question.

The firms that were about to be nationalised provide a whole new area of policy and study. In the case, for example, of the nationalisation of the *shipbuilding industry*—in part because of

Upper Clyde and its experience, the shipbuilders in the yards did not want to find that they were handed over, lock, stock and barrel, to a new nationalised shipbuilding industry which didn't take account of the spirit that they had developed in their own yards, which spirit had triggered off the decision to nationalise. Therefore, within the shipbuilding industry processes were set in motion under which the workers sat down in parallel with the new organising committee in order to work out how the industry was to be nationalised and what form of consultation and decision-making was to be created.

In the case of the *aircraft industry* the same process occurred. In this connection we should study the BAC publication on public ownership proposals produced by the workers in Bristol.[26] What they did was to think through the window-dressing of some participation and involvement schemes and to come out with a scheme which was what broadly you could call a municipal model of democracy. I am not arguing what is the best model and what is not, I am only saying that the plan for the nationalisation of the aircraft industry not only owed much of its impetus to the demand in the industry for public ownership, but also that the form such public ownership took had to reflect the desire of the people in the industry that it should be brought under an administration that was different from steel, different from the Post Office, different from coal, because those old models — whatever their merits — simply did not meet the needs of people today.

Outside the public sector and crisis situations, in the cases of Leyland, Alfred Herbert and Ferranti — three of the big rescue cases — we built into the rescue operation a direct link with the unions concerned. In the case of Ferranti, when the workers from the different plants gathered in my office after Ferranti went bust, they had never met each other before. It was the crisis that had brought them together and, if I may coin a phrase, they used the crisis to carry through their policies rather than as an excuse for postponing them. That is to say, they took the situation that confronted them and they created an organisation, within the trade union movement, that worked with the full-time officials and established cross-links by joint shop stewards' committees and consultative committees. They were realistic and recognised that you couldn't do it all at once, but they also realised that you could do it on a new basis if you really set your mind to it.

Now that has got to be the pattern for industrial planning in British industry. The whole purpose of the planning agreement is to introduce that democratic tripartite element into industrial policy. That is the unique contribution that the shop floor and Labour Movement made in the development of policy in our years of opposition. There must be open disclosure; there must be democratic planning. The guidelines, even for government policy, must be published so that people can know what is happening and not find that they wake up and discover that even a socialist government has got 'good things in store for them'—whether they like them or not.

I think that the development of a three-way relationship between the government, the trade union movement and management—I am talking about professional management—even in the nationalised industries does contain within it an ingredient absolutely lacking in old Labour thinking—at least old Labour Government thinking—and differentiates us entirely and wholly from what might otherwise seem the same when you hear a National Plan is to be developed. The relationship between the trade union movement and the government hasn't only to be shaped from the top—it must be matched and married by links between ministers and union officials, shop stewards, joint shop stewards' committees—even international links. In this connection, when I was in opposition and the aircraft industry in Bristol was worried and set up a trade union–labour liaison committee with BAC/Rolls-Royce, I said to them, 'Why don't you have a joint meeting with the people in Toulouse? If necessary why don't you get together with Toulouse and demand a joint meeting with the two ministers—the British and French ministers?' I didn't know when I said it that I would be the minister when they made that demand, and I'm very proud to say that I got the French minister to sit down with me and we met both unions and they put forward their demands for the future of the aircraft industry.

It must be international, it must have links at every level. It will involve a lot of effort and a lot of pressure from within the Labour Movement if these things are to be real, because although the government may not yet realise it, and there are many things still to be done, in the legislation that we have fought to get through Parliament there is for the first time what I would call a trigger mechanism capable of being activated by the trade union movement itself and not solely at the whim and purpose of the minister. A Labour Cabinet, even if composed entirely of members qualified to win the approval of the Institute for Workers' Control, could not, alone, do one fraction of the things that have to be done. If the Labour Movement is to play its proper role in the period of slump and depression that lies ahead, then I think we will have to be sure that the impetus for change comes continually from the movement itself.

3

Energy

Almost alone among the major industrialised countries of the West, Britain is able to look forward to total independence and self-sufficiency in energy supplies within the next year or so. On top of this we will also be net exporters of energy and the equipment that goes with it. No one should think we are entirely dependent on oil for our energy supplies. We have got 300 years of coal at our current rate of consumption. We already generate 13 per cent of our electricity by nuclear power. The British Gas Corporation is confident that the reserves available to it will last well into the next century and after that it should be possible to convert coal into synthetic natural gas. Britain is, therefore, a four-fuel economy. This is a considerable change from the 1960s when energy policy was regarded as only a peripheral interest of government. Today, with the discovery of huge quantities of oil and natural gas, on top of large reserves of coal, energy policy is now seen as central.

When I became Secretary of State for Energy in 1975, we were facing a number of outstanding issues. One concerned our relationship with the oil companies: our job was to make sure that the resources of the North Sea were exploited for the benefit of the nation as a whole and not solely for the benefit of a handful of multinationals controlled mainly from America. Then there was the question of how far and how fast we should develop our nuclear energy—and in particular whether we should establish a reprocessing plant at Windscale.

There was our decision to proceed with huge new investment in coal as a practical necessity for an industry which had sustained our manufacturing economy since the industrial revolution and upon which we shall increasingly depend. There was a need to look ahead to the day when we will no longer be able to rely on existing supplies of non-renewable energy and so we are sponsoring research into alternative sources such as wind- and wave-power. Finally, there was a need for debates on all these subjects to be conducted out in the open so that before Parliament took the final decisions we would have the benefit of the widest possible range of experience and advice. These were some of the main issues that arose from 1975 to 1979 and I want to deal with each in more detail.

North Sea Oil

Our interests in the North Sea oil are very clear national interests. They are designed to maximise the benefit to the people of the United Kingdom of the oil resources the Almighty has put around our shores, but to do it in a way that does not prevent, indeed assists as far as may be, the flow of capital into the North Sea for its development, the flow of technology that the oil companies can bring, and to try to establish a relationship with both finance and the oil companies that is on a basis of trust and confidence.

There has been no concealment in our policy. We are out to benefit as best we may the interests of the people we represent, and that should be the view of any government coming into office in the United Kingdom. That is the background against which we have developed our policy. There is a changed relationship between nation states and multinational oil companies. Perhaps I could quote a short extract from Hansard:

So the oil consumer is in rather an unusually weak position in regard to purchasing oil, because he is so easily liable to be made a forced purchaser at an artificial price. This is, of course, particularly true of a Government oil purchaser. The oil consumer has not got freedom of choice in regard to other alternative fuels, but neither has he freedom of choice in regard to the sources of supply from which he can purchase.

The speech goes on:

> We have experienced, in common with private consumers, a
> long steady squeeze by the oil trusts all over the world, and
> we have found prices and freights raised steadily against us
> until we have been pressed to pay more than double what a
> few years before we were accustomed to pay, yielding a good
> profit to the producers for the oil which was required.

That passage is dated June 17th 1914. And the speaker is
Winston Churchill, as First Lord of the Admiralty. From his
speech one can get some idea of the interests of national
security as they relate to oil. Churchill was moving the second
reading of the Bill to purchase for £2 million 51 per cent
control of the Anglo-Persian Oil Company, now British
Petroleum; the first nationalised fuel enterprise in the world,
the forerunner of OPEC state oil companies and all that followed from that. After BP came ANCAP in Uruguay in 1931
which was the second state oil company. It was Mossadegh, a
most far-sighted Iranian politician, who in 1951 set up the
National Iranian Oil Corporation.

What has happened is that there has been a shift in thinking
from the idea of oil companies as concessionaries to the idea
that they should be contractors. And this is a very important
political point. Because the relationship between governments
and oil companies are relationships between organisations in
some cases of equal strength and wealth.

If you take a comparison between the revenues of the two
largest oil companies in the world and the revenues of the two
largest oil-producing countries in the world, excluding the
Soviet Union, you will find that the revenue of Shell in 1977
was $55 billion producing 4.2 million barrels per day and the
revenue of Exxon was $58 billion producing 4.9mbpd. By
contrast the revenues of Saudi Arabia were only $38 billion
producing 9.2 million barrels per day and the revenues of Iran
were $23 billion producing 5.7mbpd. There is no doubt
whatever that the relationships between governments and oil
companies are relationships between two sets of sovereign
bodies engaged in treaty negotiations.

When Labour came to power in Britain in 1974 we found

that the arrangements with the oil companies for developing the North Sea (made in 1972) were not in the interests of the United Kingdom. The previous administration gave a very large number of licences without any provision whatsoever for any of that oil to be directed to meet United Kingdom needs. There was no legislation to start with, and there was no provision whatever in those arrangements that would guarantee to us any of the oil that might be found when the licensed blocks came to be drilled and to be explored. There was, indeed, no proper statutory framework. There was no petroleum revenue tax.

We tried to fill in those gaps, first of all by the introduction of a very complex petroleum revenue tax which differentiated between the marginal and the profitable fields and gave us an average 70 per cent return.

The second thing we did was to introduce the Petroleum and Submarine Pipelines Act which gives to any Secretary of State enormous powers over depletion and control over the fields which include, and I mention this explicitly, very considerable powers of discretion.

Third, we set up a state-owned British National Oil Corporation (BNOC) from scratch, to which we appointed as Chairman Lord Kearton, a distinguished industrialist with a long record of experience not only in industry but in working with government. At first we faced a pretty hostile atmosphere from the oil industry itself[1] which was not really ready to make available distinguished oilmen to work on BNOC. Now, however, the new corporation is a partner with the government under the participation agreements and during the mid-1980s will have access to 35 million to 45 million tonnes of oil a year, or between 700,000 and 900,000 barrels per day. With BNOC brought into being, with the Act on the statute book, and the petroleum revenue tax available to us, we sat down with the oil companies one by one to try to reach participation arrangements. We did not, and no British government would, adopt the rule of confiscation or damage the legitimate interests arising from a round of licences already agreed. Therefore we began by making it clear that the government's revenue interests would be met from taxes and royalties and not

77

through the participation agreements. What we wanted was access to the oil. We set ourselves as an objective the right to buy at market prices 51 per cent of the oil. Secondly, we sought a seat, voice and vote on the operating committees so that the British National Oil Corporation would be able to enter progressively, and slowly but steadily, into a position where it would know what was going on in the oil companies licensed in 1972. These discussions were extremely detailed, extremely difficult and we found it necessary to vary the agreements we signed to meet the different circumstances of each individual company.

We tried to inject into what were in effect treaty arrangements with them, provisions apart from access to knowledge and access to oil. One of these was that proper consultative arrangements must be set up with the companies which would both maximise the use of UK oil and maximise, as far as may be, the benefit to the United Kingdom balance of payments deriving from the oil. Multinational companies move cash and technology across the world in a way that has considerable impact on the rate of world development. Oil companies are the most dramatic example of them all, but we were not prepared to be, like the sheikhs of forty years ago, the recipients of that kind of attention without safeguarding our interests. The treaty arrangements, which we called participation agreements, were the method that we adopted. After long hours of discussion we did, with some exceptions, reach a position where almost all the major oil companies agreed.

We linked the timing of the fifth (1977) round of licences to the completion of the participation arrangements. The fifth round was deliberately made a smaller round than the 1972 round. This was because when the 1972 round was announced and the allocations were made the stress and strain upon the British industrial equipment industry was such that they were simply not in a position to meet the demand. We wanted to see as far as we could that orders for such equipment were brought to the United Kingdom in order to create jobs. About 100,000 jobs have been created in and around the oil equipment industry. In order to spread the load in a way that made possible the steady development of our own manufacturing industry, we thought that smaller and more regular rounds would be sensible. We also had in mind, of course, that smaller rounds would be a form of depletion control which did not raise the problems of cut-backs, which if introduced arbitrarily might affect the confidence of the companies that were working in the North Sea. If you go for smaller rounds, at regular intervals, you can determine how quickly you want the remaining blocks explored and hence you can adjust your oil production to some extent to meet your needs.

In the summer of 1978 we allocated sole licences to BNOC, prepared a higher tax level and stiffened the conditions for the sixth round of licences. This led to predictions that the oil companies would not find it worth their while to help us develop the North Sea. In fact applications for the sixth round of licences exceeded those for the fifth.

Our intention, like that of any oil-producing country, is that when the oil runs out, we should be left with a powerful industrial base upon which to sustain our living standards. We therefore have an intense interest in the secondary impact of oil in the United Kingdom. We are interested that the ordering of the equipment should be on the basis of full and fair opportunity. We have signed a memorandum with the oil companies, and made that memorandum a requirement of our policy, that British firms should have genuinely full and fair opportunity to bid for the equipment that is on order as a result of this major investment. There have been no difficulties about it except from the EEC. From our point of view it was right and it has pushed up the British share of this billion-pounds-a-year market from about 30 per cent to well over 50 per cent over a period of two or three years. It is bringing jobs to Scotland and other parts of the United Kingdom, and is progressively building for us an industry which will be able to meet world markets for oil equipment, particularly as the world moves to the outer-continental shelf and requires that high degree of skill in deep water drilling which we have acquired in the very difficult climate of the North Sea.

The next area to which we are giving consideration, and it is an extremely difficult problem, is the problem of depletion control. We have two or three separate factors at work which we have to take into account. One is the industrial argument which may point to a slightly slower rate of development to give our industry the time to develop to meet the market. There is also the environmental argument — which has to be taken seriously — about the sudden impact of a new technology upon the countryside and shoreline which again points to a slightly slower buildup. Then there is the argument that once you have reached self-sufficiency, if the oil supply curve rises above your forecast of domestic demand, there is a case for pushing production back so as to prolong the period of oil revenues and allow you to match your demand and supply.

We expect to be self-sufficient in oil by 1980 and this will make a considerable impact on our balance of payments. In 1976 we spent £7,000 million on oil imports. In 1977 we were producing nearly half our total needs and in the early 1980s we shall be producing around two million barrels a day which will make us self-sufficient. The total value of our oil reserves, as far as we can put a value on them, is about £170 *billion* and the British government are expecting to receive revenues to a total of about £4,000 million for all the years up to 1980 and about £3,000 million per year thereafter. Without pretending for one moment that this great legacy of oil will resolve some of the deep-seated problems that Britain has, it certainly transforms our prospects and we will acquire, well over and above the debt repayment requirements, revenues to spend for the purpose of re-industrialisation.

The Debate over Nuclear Energy

During my time as Secretary of State for Energy there were two major issues affecting the future of our nuclear programme. The first of these was whether or not Britain should go ahead and develop a fast-breeder nuclear reactor. Second, was the question of whether to proceed with plans to build a plant for reprocessing at Windscale in Cumbria.[2] The question of nuclear power is unique in human history. The problem is that we will be handing over to future generations responsibilities of monitoring and guardianship which we cannot be sure they will be in a position to discharge. If there was a plague or a war or a drought or some unforeseeable change in circumstances, we can't be sure that over the next two thousand years our descendants will be able to cope with this, and if they couldn't, the price they would have to pay would greatly affect the quality of life. That is the whole nuclear problem. If ever there was an area where open government was relevant it is this area because it is very easy in ignorance to misunderstand. As Energy Secretary I tried to make it my business to see that everything that came to me was put out for study to others. This was partly in self-defence, because if people are able to see the information that is available to the minister, if they think that that information is wrong, they will subject him to their own view. This has been criticised for being a slow process, but it is necessary.

The nuclear debate must be a mature debate between people who accept the motivation of others. To suggest that nuclear scientists were unconcerned about safety or world views on the environment would be a scandalous misrepresentation of their position. Similarly, it is equally unworthy of serious consideration to maintain that anyone who thinks that nuclear power is wrong must in some way be working for Moscow to undermine the stability of the Western world. Arguments of that kind should not be made.

We must recognise that when we are considering matters of such difficulty it is worth listening to everyone and that the pressures that are brought to bear are not — as is sometimes suggested — only those brought by the environmental lobby against the innocent nuclear power lobby. In my political life I have never known such a well-organised scientific, industrial and technical lobby as the nuclear power lobby.

The nuclear debate is not a theological dispute about the intrinsic merit of nuclear power. We are talking about electricity and how we can get it. Windscale was a case in point. If alternatives were available many people might take a different view about nuclear power. We are talking about electricity that we think we need, and we are not engaged in an argument between 'goodies' and 'baddies' because, in my opinion, both sides of this argument have contributed greatly to the debate and the decision that we now have to take.

Can anybody object to environmentalists who have insistently brought to the attention of Parliament factors of safety, problems of accidents, problems of terrorism, problems of civil liberties, problems of proliferation and, indeed, have said that we have a responsibility as stewards of the planet? Can anyone really object to nuclear scientists, who as young men may have seen Hiroshima and Nagasaki, deciding to devote their lives to 'Atoms for Peace', and for whom the whole operation of civil nuclear power is the classic case of swords into ploughshares or spears into pruning hooks? Some of the debate was conducted as though we were considering the neutron bomb, and not the use of nuclear power for civil purposes.

What we are being asked to do is to take a balanced political judgment between two known risks. One is the risk of reprocessing, which nobody in his senses could deny exists, and the other is the risk of energy shortage by relying solely on non-nuclear means. The case for Windscale is solely an energy case, and any Energy minister looking at the possibilities of meeting our demand by supply is bound to be affected more and more by the uncertainty over all fuels. How long will the oil last? Will it be interfered with by an embargo? How long will the gas last? What about the coal? Can it be obtained? How quickly can we rely upon the alternatives—and I share the view of those who argue the need to develop alternative energy —to meet our need? How much will conservation give, because it is a long programme? How easy will uranium be to get when countries that have it may well lay down conditions for its supply, as the Americans have done, and as Namibia and Australia have done? There are many political hazards there. There are also environmental hazards with all fuels as anyone who knows about the Vale of Belvoir or the Ekofisk blow-out will remember.[3] All the forecasts point to the need for a nuclear component, and this has emerged from analysis and from consultation not only in the United Kingdom; this is the view of the United States, of the Soviet Union, of the International Atomic Energy Agency and of the EEC. We must not give the impression that the only environmental factors arise from nuclear power. If you take the mining case and go in for open cast mining, it has a terrific effect on the countryside. If you're going to go for windmills, of the size planned, the effect of this, as compared to pylons which used to be much criticised by rural environment groups, is going to be formidable. If you're going to build the Severn barrage, which will cost £4,000 million, probably twice as much as the fast-breeder reactor, the impact of this on the ecology of the Severn basin is unpredictable. So we should not give the impression that it's only nuclear power which has environmental hazards. But there are special dangers arising from the long life of nuclear waste, and the risk of the proliferation of nuclear weapons. All you can do is to bring them out into the open, publish everything you know, let people reach a view, and in the end the minister has to be responsible to Parliament and the electors for the final decision that he makes. Regarding safety, it is not only nuclear energy that could prove dangerous. From 1947 to 1976 8,001 miners were killed underground and 49,971 seriously injured in the UK, while in the nuclear industry there has been nothing like the same number. Another example is that over the same period 200,000 people have been killed by the motor car and 9 million injured. Had there been a Select Committee to consider whether a new piece of technology known as the motor car was to be approved and someone had been able to predict confidently that in the next thirty years it would kill 200,000 people and injure 9 million, Parliament might not have approved it. I do not want to suggest that there are acceptable levels of accidents or safety. I do not mean that at all. I mean that there are problems with all technologies; and we have to recognise that the nuclear argument is not about the current safety level but about future potential, the development of which we cannot, in all fairness, foresee. Of course the risk of accident cannot be brushed aside. Of course the risk of terrorism cannot be put out of mind, or, if the risk of terrorism is to be minimised, the impact upon civil liberties which that would involve cannot be put out of mind. In my view the most powerful argument is the argument about proliferation of nuclear weapons as an accidental by-product of the uncontrolled spread of sensitive nuclear technology intended solely for civil purposes. We are doing everything possible to prevent this by international agreement, supervision and control. The question is not whether these are valid points because, of course, they are valid points. The question is whether they are so decisive as to justify overturning the basic energy policy, with all the risks.

I greatly resent those who say that either we have a civilised society with energy consumption or we go back to the tent and the candle, and that this is the difference between the nuclear and non-nuclear schools. This is not true. If we are sensible, we are choosing between a wide range of possible scenarios. There is a wide range of choices. The conventional wisdom is that coal, conservation and nuclear power is the right mix, but the exact balance between them and alternative sources, as well as the impact of combined heat and power or anything else which may come through, must be looked at carefully.

If we look ahead to the mix of fuels which we think we shall need in this country in the year 2000, it is not possible to abstract the nuclear component without running a serious risk which no Energy minister could recommend. That is the argument which has to be presented.

If for the best reasons in the world the case against nuclear power were to prevail, our energy policy as it has developed by general agreement would have to be completely recast. British industry would be greatly affected, the self-sufficiency upon which we rest so much would no longer be assured, and the economic consequences of seeking to import energy to replace the nuclear power would transform our long-term economic prospects. How should the question be decided? Some would say that it is a matter for the experts. Others say that it is for officials. Others say that it is for the Cabinet, where decisions of this kind have always been made in the past, behind the closed curtains of the Official Secrets Act. In my view, however, decisions on such important matters should be made only after the fullest public debate with all the facts made public.

Windscale

In the case of the Windscale reprocessing plant, we decided that the House of Commons should make the final decision because it was essentially a question of political judgment.

Since the government were involved in handling this matter over a long period it is only fair to set the chronology upon the record. The proposal from British Nuclear Fuels, which included building a Thermal Oxide Reprocessing Plant (THORP) to deal with waste from Japan and other countries as well as the UK, came to me first in September 1975. The Cabinet discussed it. BNFL had two public meetings, one in Cumbria and one in London, in order to ensure that the case was understood. I went to Tokyo to discuss with the Japanese Government arrangements under which the waste would be returned.

In March 1976 I announced the government's decision, that in their view it was all right. Then, in December, after a great deal of public discussion and after the responsibility for waste management had been transferred to the Department of the Environment, the inquiry was set up.[4] The inquiry went on from June to November 1977, the report came out the following January, we had our debate in March, the recommendations were accepted and the decision to go ahead at Windscale was taken by the House of Commons in May 1978.

No one in his senses could describe all this as a charade. We encouraged discussion and many other bodies besides the House of Commons—the churches, other institutions, political parties, trade unions and so on—joined in the debate. We provided an opportunity for the arguments to be put. We sought independent advice from the Parker Commission, we joined in the international talks, and deferred the decision for two years.

The disappointment of the environmentalists that their view on Windscale did not prevail was understandable, but the issues they raised will always be on the agenda. There will be a large number of stages at which Parliament reviews the progress of the plant at Windscale; there will be many other opportunities for further projects to be examined with the same detailed scrutiny as we applied to Windscale. One such case is the future of the fast-breeder reactor.

The Fast Breeder

This is the next stage in the development of civil nuclear

power. No decision to proceed with this will be made until it has been subjected to independent scrutiny in the way that the Windscale project was.

Nuclear technology has considerable implications for democracy and before we proceed any further we must look at the need for democratic control in the light of the following considerations: first, its close connection with military policy in regard to the development of nuclear weapons which are the most sophisticated technology available, the most dangerous and the one covered by the greatest secrecy. In Britain we developed nuclear weapons secretly without parliamentary knowledge or approval.

Second, the link between the military and the civil use of nuclear technology makes it a matter of great public concern. The production of plutonium, the development of enrichment and reprocessing, all carry an attendant risk of proliferation or vulnerability to terrorism. These are also reasons for shrouding civil nuclear processes under conditions of top secrecy.

Third, the wide gap between expert understanding and public knowledge of nuclear matters which is used to justify the exclusion of laymen—even members of Parliament and ministers are laymen for that purpose—from the knowledge of what is really going on for fear that they might not understand.

Fourth, the high rate of spending, even in civil nuclear technology, creates powerful vested interests in the industries that live upon those budgets.

I must say that I have the highest possible regard for the skill, expertise and public spiritedness of all those who work in and around the atomic industry.

What I now want to say is not a criticism, but is a comment upon the implications for democracy of the use of a technology as complex as nuclear power.

The information necessary for democratic control is not as readily available as it should be. Here are some concrete examples that have caused me concern, over a period of nearly thirteen years as a minister with responsibility for nuclear power.

Around 1957 there was a major Soviet nuclear accident. It

was later announced by Dr Roy Medvedev, a Soviet scientist, and became the subject of public comment. This was known at the time to the United States authorities and afterwards to the UK Atomic Energy Authority but I understand that the Cabinet was not informed.

In 1968, or thereabouts, 200 tons of uranium then under the safeguards of Euratom disappeared and were thought to have gone to Israel. This very important matter was also known and understood by the atomic authorities at the time, but was not reported to the Cabinet or the minister most concerned.

In 1969 there was a problem of corrosion in the Magnox power stations. If the bolts that had become corroded had fallen into the reactors it might not have been possible to shut them down. I was informed at the time but there was very strong pressure not to reveal the full extent of this problem for fear of creating alarm.

From that moment I insisted that every single incident, however minor, at every nuclear power station in the United Kingdom was to be reported personally to me, and I invited Sir Alec Merrison of Bristol University to set up an inquiry into these circumstances.

In 1970 a contract was signed with Rio Tinto Zinc at Rossing in Namibia before the Cabinet had been informed.[5] In 1976 there were two major leaks at Windscale; some weeks had elapsed before their full extent was brought to my attention.

The last example relates to nuclear waste disposal. The environmentalists have a very strong case when they argue that the public were never informed that the technology to process, by vitrification, highly toxic nuclear waste has not yet, even now, been fully perfected.

Information is the key to democratic control. The publishing of information, except for sensitive technical data which might encourage the spread of nuclear weapons or make terrorism easier, must be regarded as the heart of democratic government.

If I am very doubtful about the fast-breeder reactor, as I am, and believe that any proposal to build one should be delayed, as I do, it is because I am not yet satisfied that our democratic machinery is strong enough to control this new development and not because I doubt the technical competence of those in the industry to construct and operate one. The central question is, is it possible that technology which was intended to permit man to control his environment becomes the instrument by which man is more fully controlled by his environment? One can argue that in terms of ideology. Is not the real answer that when we become so dependent on high technology—it could be oil, gas or a single ball-bearing company producing all the ball bearings in Europe—we may actually be creating a situation in which what we thought would be liberation is really vulnerability, what we thought would be freedom actually endangers liberty, and that in order to safeguard ourselves against the threat of interruption of those essential supplies that are themselves centralised we have to give up essential political liberties? Churchill made a speech at the time when the chamber of the House of Commons was being rebuilt after being bombed by Hitler. He said: 'In the beginning we shape our institutions and in the end they shape us.' It is the same with the technology that we handle. In the beginning we shape our technology, but if we are not very careful in the end it will shape us. It is for the democratic process to operate to see that it does not do so in a way that damages our central rights and liberties. There is no issue more urgent than the democratic control of nuclear power.

A Future for Coal

There was a time in the 1960s when governments took for granted that coal was a declining industry. Against the advice of the mineworkers' union investment was allowed to decline, there were widespread pit closures and little or no effort was put into discovering new reserves of coal.[6] It wasn't until the oil-producing nations suddenly quadrupled the price of their oil in the early 1970s that the folly of neglecting the coal industry was brought home forcibly. We have now turned our back on the years of decline in the coal industry. The British people paid heavily for those mistakes and those mistakes must not be repeated. In 1974 the Labour Government approved the 'Plan for Coal' and set up the Tripartite Committee which was a historic turning point for the industry. In this committee the mining unions, the managers of the National Coal Board and ministers, not only Energy ministers but also Treasury and other interested ministers, sat down together to plan the recovery of coal.

In 1976 the Coal Board came forward with 'Coal for the Future', aiming at a production target of 170 million tons by the year 2000; ambitious plans that would require something like four million tons of new capacity a year, involving an investment in mining of around £475 million a year.

By July 1978, 125 major projects had been started, involving over £1,000 million of investment. New pits had been started at Selby, Royston and Betwys. Through exploration 2,000 million tons of economically recoverable coal have been discovered over this four-year period — a rate of discovery that runs at four times the rate of consumption of coal over this period. Although oil may get the headlines, coal is the solid achievement in discovery and in prospects.[7]

As regards the social side of our responsibilities to the coal industry, the 1975 Coal Industry Act set up a scheme to compensate those miners suffering from pneumoconiosis — dust on the lung. Nearly 65,000 successful claims were made under this scheme in the first three years after the Act became law. We also introduced an earlier retirement scheme for miners, allowing those eligible with long experience of face work to retire at sixty.

In 1977 we passed a Coal Industry Act which raised the borrowing limits of the Coal Board, enabling them to extend their investment in new projects and to make better provision for their employees. The Act also widened the powers of the Coal Board allowing it to mine other minerals, to operate overseas and to move into petrochemicals. We have also made available funds to finance the making of oil and gas from coal so that we are prepared for the day when the oil and the gas run out.

In July 1978, at the miners' union's annual conference at Torquay, a planning agreement, the first of its kind between a nationalised industry and the government, was signed.[8] Under this the government, the Coal Board and the union will meet regularly to plan the future of the industry as part of an integrated national energy policy. The coal industry is now set upon a path of expansion.

Alternative Sources of Energy

Finally, there is the question of what happens when the oil, gas and even coal begin to run out. Sir Brian Flowers in his report on nuclear power and the risks to the environment criticised the lack of research into renewable energy resources; so did the Parliamentary Select Committee on Science and Technology.[9] The government accepted these criticisms. We have now got a £10 million programme covering solar, wind and wave methods of producing energy. We are going to have a new examination of the Severn barrage project to see what the costs and benefits would be.[10] So far all this is on a small scale. The big money comes at the development and manufacturing stage, and the cost of research to identify alternatives is minuscule compared to the cost of actually building power stations. We are definitely going to give this a greater degree of priority, but I can't see it playing an enormous role within the next twenty years. Once we have a wave system that will work, and make up our minds about the Severn barrage, then the rate of spending could, of course, be increased substantially, if it makes sense to do so. And of course, in the long run, benign and renewable alternative sources have tremendous advantages in that they don't deplete the world's scarce raw materials and they leave oil and coal to be used as a feedstock and for manufacturing purposes, so you don't waste them by burning them. Alternative energies will develop more rapidly as soon as we have got absolutely certain schemes that we know will really provide energy needs on a basis that is appropriate to our demand. Then the whole argument will change towards greater funding of them. It is against that possibility that we must be sure we do not pre-empt too many of the limited resources we have at our disposal.

Nor should we assume that a lower level of energy consumption would necessarily be in the general interest. It could have implications for employment and the standard of living. We have to be careful that we don't accidentally back into solving the energy crisis by a permanent slump.

Conventional energy wisdom owes something to the fact that there are a few vested interests lurking about who come along with an energy crisis in one hand and a solution in their hip pocket. We should be very sceptical of those who tell us that something terrible is about to happen, and then produce their plan to put it right so you don't have to worry any more.

Conclusion

It is impossible to separate energy from the national interest. It is also impossible to separate energy policy, and the investment that goes with it, from the needs of economic growth and this particularly applies to a country like the United Kingdom. Over a long period, we have seen the effect of progressive under-investment on our capacity to compete internationally in industrial production. Of course there are other problems too but the steady erosion of the manufacturing capacity of the oldest manufacturing nation in the world (we in Britain have been industrialised for six or seven generations), and the present waste of skill involved in that erosion is really nothing short of tragic for a country like ours. It began, you could argue, in the 1880s when German steel production overtook British steel production. You could give all sorts of excuses like the effect of two world wars. You can blame it on anything you like, national malaise or reds under the bed.

If you're in Scotland, you can say it's due to the English. If you're in the Midlands you can claim it's due to the blacks. You name it, somebody's got a scapegoat. But whatever the reason is, it cannot go on. It is absolutely essential, not only that we should provide through energy investment some lift in our investment in the United Kingdom, but that the energy revenues should be used to finance re-industrialisation. We must also face up to the problem of unemployment which is a much more serious problem than most people in authority in the West now seem to think. There are many factors that contribute to rising unemployment. Lack of competitiveness

may knock a firm out. Re-equipment may produce technological redundancy. So may the arrival on the labour market
of more young people who seek jobs after having been through
a good educational system. Welfare or unemployment pay is
not an answer to the problems of unemployment. Unemployment may not present itself to us in the way in which it did in
the 1930s when the hunger marchers came from Jarrow to
London, but it presents itself in all sorts of other ways that are
very evident. Unemployment can produce racial tensions of a
kind that even I remember from watching Oswald Mosley and
the Blackshirts going through the streets of London before the
war. Energy investment is not only a means to new energy
supply or the conservation of existing supplies, but a definite
contribution to transforming Britain's whole economic fortunes.

4

The EEC

Apart from a short period during the end of the 1966–70 Wilson Government I have been an opponent of British membership of the Common Market for the best part of twenty years. In 1963 when I was approached by the magazine *Encounter* for my views on Mr Macmillan's first attempt to get Britain into the EEC, I listed the following as the issues which had to be considered:

First, that the Treaty of Rome which entrenches *laissez-faire* as its philosophy and chooses its bureaucracy as its administrative method will stultify effective national economic planning without creating the necessary supranational planning mechanisms for growth and social justice under democratic control.

Second, that the political inspiration of the EEC amounts to a belief in the institutionalisation of NATO which will harden the division of Europe, and encourage the emergence of a new nuclear super-power, thus worsening East–West relations and making disarmament more difficult.

Third, that the trading policy which the community will inevitably pursue will damage the exports of underdeveloped countries and increase the speed at which the gulf between rich and poor countries is widening.

Fourth, that on balance Britain would have less influence on world events if she were inside than she could have if she remained outside.

Fifth, that experience shows that written constitutions

entrenching certain interests and principles are virtually impossible to alter.[1]

It was not until 1968 that, as Minister of Technology, I justified the decision of the then Labour Government to apply for membership of the EEC, although I argued within the government that the consent of the British people would need to be obtained:

> Britain may have been slow to see the importance of the European Communities. But I believe that she was the first to see that technology imposes on us all the inexorable logic of scale ... The full benefits of an integrated European technology can only be achieved when Britain is a member of the EEC.[2]

But in parallel with that argument it became clear that this was a democratic issue and after the Wilson Government decided to apply for EEC membership I wrote to my constituents in Bristol setting out the case for a referendum on British entry. In the summer of 1971 my constituency party launched a campaign to persuade the Labour Party to adopt the referendum as official policy and I presented a Private Member's Bill to the House of Commons setting out how a referendum could be organised.

In March 1972 President Pompidou announced that a referendum would be held in France to let the French people express their attitude on the question of British entry. This helped to tip the scales within the National Executive of the Labour Party and the shadow cabinet in favour of a British referendum. In October 1972 the Labour Party conference officially endorsed the call for a referendum.

Four months later, on January 1st 1973, the Conservative Government under Mr Edward Heath took Britain into the Common Market by a simple majority vote in Parliament. The British people were subjected to the European Commission and the Treaty of Rome by a Prime Minister who signed the Treaty using the royal prerogative without seeking the endorsement of the British people. He then forced the necessary legislation through Parliament, including a provision that

Community law was for ever to be directly enforceable in the United Kingdom without any form of parliamentary approval, thus intending to exclude the electors thereafter from exercising any influence on such laws through the use of the ballot box.

The Labour Party therefore promised at its 1973 conference that a future Labour government would seek to renegotiate the terms of the treaty of accession and then hold a referendum on continued membership. Labour Governments were subsequently returned to power in February and October 1974 and the referendum was arranged for June 1975.

During the six weeks that led up to Referendum Day Cabinet ministers were released from the unanimity convention and were allowed to campaign for either proposition. A number of Cabinet ministers campaigned to end our membership of the EEC and in this section I shall try to set out my main arguments for doing so. These divide roughly under three headings: the loss of political self-determination; loss of control over the United Kingdom's industry and trade; and the closely related question of increasing unemployment.

Loss of Political Self-determination

The European Community has set itself the objectives of developing a common foreign policy, a form of common nationality expressed through a common passport, a directly elected assembly, and an economic and monetary union which, taken together, would in effect make the United Kingdom into one province of a Western European state. Continued membership of the Community would, therefore, mean the end of Britain as a completely self-governing nation and of our democratically elected Parliament as the supreme law-making body of the United Kingdom.

The parliamentary democracy we have developed and established in Britain is based, not upon the sovereignty of Parliament, but upon the sovereignty of the people, who, by exercising their vote, lend their sovereign powers to members of Parliament, to use on their behalf for the duration of a single Parliament only—powers that must be returned intact to the electorate to whom they belong, to lend again to the members

95

of Parliament they elect in each subsequent general election. Five basic democratic rights derive from this relationship, and each of them is fundamentally altered by Britain's membership of the European Community.

First, parliamentary democracy means that every man and woman over eighteen is entitled to vote to elect his or her member of Parliament to serve in the House of Commons, and the consent of the House of Commons is necessary before Parliament can pass any Act laying down new laws or imposing new taxation upon the people. British membership of the Community subjects us all to laws and taxes which members of Parliament do not enact. Instead such laws and taxes are enacted by authorities not directly elected and who cannot be dismissed through the ballot box.

Second, parliamentary democracy means that members of Parliament who derive their powers directly from the British people can change any law and any tax by majority vote. British membership of the Community means that Community laws and taxes cannot be repealed or changed by the British Parliament, but only by Community authorities not directly elected by the British people.

Third, parliamentary democracy means that British courts and judges must uphold all laws passed by Parliament, and if Parliament changes any law the courts must enforce the new law because it has been passed by Parliament which has been directly elected by the people. British membership of the Community requires the British courts to uphold and enforce Community laws that have not been passed by Parliament, and that Parliament cannot change or amend, even when such laws conflict with laws passed by Parliament, since Community law overrides British law.

Fourth, parliamentary democracy means that all British governments, ministers, and the civil servants under their control, can only act within the laws of Britain and are accountable to Parliament for everything they do, and hence Parliament is accountable to the electors as a whole. British membership of the Community imposes upon British governments duties and constraints not deriving from the British Parliament, and thus in discharging those duties ministers are not accountable to Parliament or to the British people who elect them.

Fifth, parliamentary democracy, because it entrenches the rights of the people to elect and dismiss members of Parliament, also secures the continuing accountability of members of Parliament to the electorate, obliging members of Parliament to listen to the expression of the British people's views at all times, between, as well as during, general elections, and thus offers a continuing possibility of peaceful change through Parliament to meet the people's needs. British membership of the Community, by permanently transferring sovereign legislative and financial powers to Community authorities, who are not directly elected by the British people, also permanently insulates those authorities from direct control by the British electors who cannot dismiss them and whose views therefore need carry no weight with them and whose grievances they cannot be compelled to remedy.

In short, the power of the electors of Britain, through their direct representatives in Parliament, to make laws, levy taxes, change laws which the courts must uphold, and control the conduct of public affairs, has been substantially ceded to the European Community whose Council of Ministers and Commission are neither collectively elected nor collectively dismissed by the British people, nor even by the peoples of all the Community countries put together.

These five rights have protected us in Britain from the worst abuse of power by government, safeguarded us against the excesses of bureaucracy, defended our basic liberties, offered us the prospect of peaceful change, reduced the risk of civil strife, and bound us together by creating a national framework of consent for all the laws under which we were governed.

It is sometimes supposed that the formation of a fully fledged United States of Western Europe — for that is what the Common Market was intended by its founders to become — is inspired by the same principles and ideals as motivated those who established the United States of America. There is no real parallel.

The United States was dedicated to the idea of democratic self-government and it has, ever since, steadily developed and extended that ideal of democracy in all its political institutions. Every man or woman in the United States of America enjoys the right to elect his or her congressman and senator and to vote to remove them from office, in order to change the law. By contrast, within the European Community many of these same legislative and fiscal powers are exercised by thirteen appointed commissioners who are neither elected by, nor accountable to, the peoples in the nine countries in which their laws apply and are enforced through the courts. These commissioners and their staffs, although appointed by member governments, are not their representatives, and do not accept instructions from them.

The nine-man Council of Ministers, on which Britain has one representative, can generally act only on a proposal put to it by the Commission, and the Council can, in law, only amend the Commission's proposed legislation by a unanimous vote of all the Council of Ministers. The Commission can legislate without reference to the Council on some topics. Community legislation, by regulation, overrides the decisions of all the elected Parliaments of the nine countries and even their national constitutions. What other body of men in the Western world enjoys so much political power as the European Commission enjoys over the lives of so many people and without a shred of direct accountability to those people for the use they may make of their power? The constitution of the United States has nothing to compare with the European Commission.

On the other hand, it was argued that there were compensating features for Britain in the proposed new arrangements. The pooling of sovereignty, for example, was held to produce increased national freedom because of increased economic strength. Union with the Community, it was suggested, was a passport of entry into the world's largest trading bloc, while pursuit of that Victorian chimera of independent self-government would lead to disaster.

The British people were told they had no choice; that they were too weak to stand alone and that if Britain left the EEC they would suffer a catastrophic economic crisis; that ideas of national self-determination were out of date. These arguments were perhaps used at the time of American independence in

1776 too, and it may have been such arguments that Benjamin Franklin had in mind when he said: 'They that can give up essential liberty to obtain a little temporary safety deserve neither liberty nor safety.'[3]

The 1975 referendum was a direct challenge to the claim, even from a democratically elected House of Commons, of the right to give away, for ever, the independence of our country and the liberties of the people, both of which it held merely in trust for the electorate which elected it. Only the British people had the moral authority to decide whether to retain their full power of democratic self-government or approve its permanent surrender to the Common Market Commission, in return for such benefits as it might be thought would follow.

Loss of Control over the United Kingdom's Industry and Trade

At the time of the referendum campaign I was Secretary of State for Industry and therefore had a particularly strong interest in the effects of entry on Britain's industrial future. As we have already seen, Labour had been elected in 1974 on an industrial programme which called for considerable state intervention in industry in order to restore production and investment. As a result of our entry into the EEC every key decision in the fields of industrial and regional policy would be subject to supervision, control and a possible veto by the Commission.

Take the example of steel. Under the Treaty of Paris which set up the European Coal and Steel Community, we have lost the power to control investment, mergers and prices in the steel industry — even though British Steel is a nationalised concern. I was told this bluntly in Brussels.

Or take shipbuilding and aircraft. The investment programme of the nationalised shipbuilding industry would be equally subject to the approval of the Commission. Proposals to expand shipbuilding capacity would have to be considered by them in the context of the European shipbuilding industry. The same applies to the new aircraft corporation.

As regards regional policy, although the Commission initially gave Britain a three-year licence to continue with existing policy, it has reaffirmed its own powers under the Treaty of Rome; powers which can be enforced against the British government through the courts.

Regarding industrial policy, every major proposal for state aid to assist investment in manufacturing industry — whether for British Leyland, Ferranti or even workers' co-operatives — would be subject to the approval of the Commission.

Finally, I called at the time of the referendum for those in favour of continuing British membership to answer certain key questions as to who would control our off-shore oil resources which were at that time valued at around £100,000 million. Would there be a Common Market energy policy and what would it mean for North Sea oil and gas? Would the Commission assume control over the rate at which these resources were depleted? Would the Treaty of Rome apply to the continental shelf? Would Britain be allowed to discriminate in favour of home-based industries by permitting them access to the oil at more favourable prices than we charge for exporting it?

Later, as Secretary of State for Energy, I began to discover for myself the answers to some of these questions. By July 1978 we had no less than three commissioners chasing us on various aspects of our energy policy. First there was Commissioner Brunner,[4] who wanted the Commission to take charge of our refinery policy. This would have had the effect of unlocking the multinational oil companies from the relationships they have negotiated with the British government. Commissioner Brunner also wanted to take responsibility for nuclear decisions so that instead of, for example, Mr Justice Parker holding an inquiry into the fast-breeder reactor we will wake up to discover the Commission have decided we will have a fast breeder, no matter what we want. If I went to the House of Commons and said that whatever you think, and whatever I think and whatever Mr Justice Parker thinks, we have got to build a fast-breeder reactor, it would shatter the relationship of trust and confidence between the government and the nuclear industry and the people concerned with environmental issues.

Commissioner Vouel, in charge of Competition Policy, was

quick to assert that our interest relief grants, which have given us 60 per cent of the £1-billion-a-year market for equipment in Scotland and the North East and where 100,000 jobs have been created, are contrary to the Treaty of Rome and announced on May 2nd 1979, the eve of the general election, that it is illegal to continue with them. And when he visited me Commissioner Vouel said he thought that the monopoly purchase of gas from the North Sea by British Gas might be contrary to the Treaty of Rome. If it were illegal to buy all the gas, the whole energy balance in the United Kingdom would be disturbed. Next there was M. Davignon, the Industrial Commissioner, who was looking at two other aspects of our energy policy. One was the landing requirement under which we say if you discover oil in the North Sea it has to be landed in the United Kingdom. If it were no longer possible for us to require the oil to be landed in Britain then, of course, a central part of the oil policy would have been transferred from this country to the Commission. Commissioner Davignon has also challenged the role of the Offshore Supplies Office in trying to get work for British industry on a 'full and fair opportunity' basis.

All these events raise very big issues. There is in the whole area of energy policy a creeping competence under which the Commission begin with an innocuous resolution, for example to contain the dangers of nuclear waste, and before you know where you are the whole thing has moved from London or Bonn to Paris or Brussels. Quite apart from the other issues, all this has considerable implications for the level of employment in Britain.

Unemployment and the EEC

During the referendum campaign those of us who were against entry argued that it would lead to even greater unemployment than that forced upon us by the world recession. We predicted that in the long run our membership of the EEC would result in mass unemployment and the increasing emigration of our workers and their families to the continent in search of jobs. Nothing that has happened since that time leads me to revise that view.

Mr Heath and those who led the pro-European campaign gave no hint that they understood the horrifying possibility that for the British people EEC membership could mean inhabiting a group of European offshore islands whose industry is permanently unable to provide the jobs and national income to support them. Yet the Treaty of Rome enshrines the essential principles of Selsdon economics which Mr Heath tried in 1970–71 with such disastrous results. The treaty has no commitment to maintain full employment in any member country. The absence of this commitment combined with the treaty provisions for free movement of labour and capital provides a chilling insight into the probable economic fate of the United Kingdom in Europe.

The Commission, like the Conservatives, understands that industry in the British regions is regrettably weak. The Commission, again like the Conservatives, believes it wrong in principle to protect lame ducks. Redundant British workers will be expected to move to expanding continental enterprises which need their skilled labour. Should Britain remain in Europe this philosophy could lead the Commission, as inevitably as it led Mr Heath, to the sort of confrontation with organised labour that we had in Britain in 1973–74. British workers will not accept the suffering caused by this destructive and mechanistic industrial philosophy.

The Common Market's industrial policy is based on a very simple and well-understood concept: survival of the fittest. They believe that industrial enterprises are engaged in a competition for the right to survive, a competition which eliminates the weak and ensures that only healthy and vigorous enterprises continue. The duty of the Commission is to make certain that nothing interferes with this competition. Article Three of the Treaty of Rome is unambiguous. It provides for the elimination of all barriers to internal trade, the prohibition of any distortions to competition and the free movement of persons, services and capital throughout the Community.

Supranational powers are allocated to Community institutions and member states are required to accept major limitations on their freedom lest they obstruct the process of competition.

The difficulty for Britain is that our enterprises are weak and under this system many will not survive. Continental manufacturers are far better equipped, achieve a much higher level of productivity and have a much firmer hold in world markets than our own ill-equipped and depressed industrial establishments. Already we are heavy net importers from the rest of the Community in two large industrial sectors—steel and cars. Most other branches of manufacturing have also been feeling the pressure of intense European competition and are losing their traditional markets far quicker than they can find footholds in new ones. The picture presented by industrial surveys in Britain is of occasional successes against a background of almost uniform failure. Whereas high unemployment in other parts of the Community has been a sharp and temporary reaction to the oil crisis, recession, redundancy and closure, in Britain it is establishing itself as a worsening trend.

From the standpoint of Mr Heath and the pro-Marketeers this almost unthinkable decline in our national fortunes should be regarded only as a transitional problem reflecting the profound alterations needed to rationalise the economic structure of Western Europe as a whole. Industrial contraction in Britain would be the natural and necessary price to be paid for the creation of an integrated and prosperous Western European economic system, leading to a full political federation.

Effective national measures to reverse Britain's decline would be unacceptable to the Community, for they would totally undermine the principles on which it is based. Even our share of the pitifully meagre regional fund comes from our money channelled back under their control. Neither the Commission nor other member states could allow Britain to destroy the free market they have taken fifteen years to achieve.

Many of those who advocated the submerging of Britain within such a Common Market believed that in some magical fashion European prosperity would overflow into the United Kingdom. Certainly, for British shareholders of European companies, and for administrators and managers who hope to be put on European pay scales, that may be true. But for working people this is not true. For many the choice will be between unemployment in Britain and a job on the continent.

At the height of the referendum campaign in May 1975 something of an uproar was caused by my estimate that about half a million jobs had been lost in Britain as a result of the growing deficit in manufacturing trade between the UK and our (at that time) six Common Market partners. My estimate, based on official overseas trade statistics, concerned the value net deficit of imports over exports in areas such as machinery, textiles, steel and chemicals, and involved translating these into the number of jobs that could have been created by making the same goods in Britain. The total number of jobs lost in this way, based on figures for January to March 1975, was about 137,000. We then calculated (using the foreign trade multiplier) the secondary reduction in employment which would result from this trade deficit with the Community, which gave us an additional figure of 360,000 lost jobs. This was the basis for my estimate of half a million unemployed, who at that time might have been in employment but for our trade deficit with the EEC.

Since then the situation has grown considerably worse. Just how bad can be gleaned from Table 4 which shows the widening gap in manufacturing trade between Britain and the EEC for the period 1970–77.[5]

Table 4

Year	£ million Balance of total trade with EEC Six	£ million Balance of trade in manufactured goods with EEC Six
1970	— 65	+ 161
1971	— 180	+ 84
1972	— 493	— 198
1973	—1,122	— 584
1974	—2,063	— 993
1975	—2,177	— 962
1976	—2,408	—1,093
1977	—2,346	—1,399

This large imbalance in our trade with the EEC Six is not, however, reflected in our trade with the rest of the world. Indeed, our surplus on trade in manufactured goods with the rest of the world (i.e. the non-Six) has risen from £2,073 million in 1970 to £6,881 million in 1977, and has increased further in the first three months of 1978.[6]

This is extremely important because when we were taken into the market we were told by Mr Heath and his ministers, not to mention most of our newspapers, that membership of the EEC would mean that we would sell more goods than we bought, and create jobs in Britain. In fact the opposite has happened. We have bought substantially more goods from the EEC than we have sold, and lost jobs in Britain.

After the Referendum

Unfortunately, in spite of these arguments, those of us who campaigned against Britain remaining in the Common Market did not succeed in convincing the majority of the British people to support our point of view. The result of the referendum was an almost two to one majority in favour of remaining in the EEC. I believe our failure was mainly due to the enormous strength of the forces ranged against us. These included the majority of the Labour Cabinet, the entire leadership of the Conservative Party, all but one of our national newspapers and the entire business community. They had enormous funds and other resources at their disposal.[7] However, in common with all those who campaigned for the referendum, I promised to accept the verdict.

But, as I also said at the time, British policy towards the Common Market would feature prominently in all our future domestic political discussions and in all future general elections. In these political discussions at home we are bound to take account of what has happened during our membership, not all of which, of course, can properly be attributed to the EEC. The published figures show:

1 That British consumers and taxpayers are paying heavily for the Common Agricultural Policy, partly in its subsidies to European farmers and partly in higher food prices.[8]

2 That our accumulated trade deficit with the original six EEC countries, during our first five years of membership, amounted to over £10,000 million, of which half was in manufactured goods. In 1977 alone our trade deficit with the original EEC six amounted to nearly £2½ billion.[9]

3 That earlier expectations of more jobs being created as a result of our membership had not materialised—indeed unemployment had risen steadily. Partly, of course, because of the world slump.

4 That in the first three years of membership nearly four times as much British capital (£1,034 million) was invested in the EEC as was invested by the EEC (£296 million) in the UK.[10]

5 That during our membership Britain's living standards have actually declined relative to the average living standards throughout the Community; and the gap between the richer Community countries and the poorer countries of the EEC (including Britain) is steadily widening.

6 That over the five years up to 1982 Britain was expected to pay nearly £5,800 million to the Community budget over and above its expected receipts from that Community budget.[11]

Given that this is so, I feel that in retrospect we were right to raise these issues in the way that we did during the period leading up to the referendum. Although our views were the object of ridicule by a large section of the press and the business and political establishment, I believe that history will treat us more kindly. It is comforting to know that I am not entirely alone in this view. This, for example, is what the BBC Common Market correspondent, John Simpson, had to say only eighteen months after the referendum:

The great debate, so-called, which ended with the 1975 referendum seems a very dead affair now ... Looking back at the speeches of the time, one is struck by how few of the prophecies made so freely have actually come to anything and how scarcely anyone forecast what has happened. Some people did. Mr Tony Benn, for instance, comes out of this test by hindsight rather well, and so does Mr Peter Shore. Unemployment and our trade deficit have reached the kind of levels the two men said they would.[12]

We are bound to consider our future relations with the EEC in the light of our experience of membership. Four alternative responses to this situation have been publicly canvassed. Firstly, to go on as we have, doing our best to make the Community policies more responsive to our needs and to seek changes of policy where necessary, as in agriculture. This was the clear policy of the 1974–79 Labour Government.

Secondly, we could press for a United States of Europe with wider powers for the Community over the UK, converting Britain into an island province of a federal European state, governed from Brussels under the Treaty of Rome.

Thirdly, we could campaign for a fundamental and democratic reform of Britain's relations with the Common Market through the British Parliament, by amending the European Communities Act. Among such reforms would be basic changes in the Common Agricultural Policy, the restoration of parliamentary control over British ministers who attend the Council of Ministers in Brussels, and over all regulations, directives and decisions made by the Council and the Commission, which the House of Commons could then accept, reject or amend at will.

The fourth view that has been canvassed is to persuade the British people to leave the Common Market altogether, as we have a clear constitutional right to do if Parliament and the British people so decide.

These alternatives are likely to receive further study and the British people will ultimately have to decide between them. In my view if fundamental reform is not achieved within a reasonable period, we will have to consider very seriously whether continued British membership of the Common Market is in the interests of our country.

5

Democracy

Parliamentary democracy and the party system have in recent years been criticised not only for their inability to solve some of our problems but also for their failure to reflect others adequately. It is not only some members of the public who are disenchanted. There are people inside active politics, of whom I am one, who have long felt uneasy, and who believe that the alienation of Parliament from the people constitutes a genuine cause for concern. Political debates concentrating on economic and other management issues between government and opposition (whether Labour or Conservative) sometimes appear to blank out everything else, while a number of other issues are not sufficiently discussed because they have not been fitted into the current pattern of political debate. This section looks at some of these issues. It begins with a brief analysis of the way in which technological change has, on the one hand, given rise to bigger and more centralised units of production or bureaucracy, and on the other hand, given rise to demands by individuals for greater control over the decisions which affect their daily lives. It then goes on to suggest some ways in which government can be made more accountable to Parliament and to the people.

Technology and Democracy

We can safely leave aside the scientific principles that have made technological advance possible and confine our attention to the result of their application. It is not how modern technology works that concerns us, as citizens, but what effect it has had on life. If we try to quantify the advances technology has made in the last fifty years, in terms of sheer machine capability, we can get an idea of the pace of that change, and what it has meant.

In 1920 an aircraft flew at 100 miles per hour for the first time; in 1945 the first jet passed the sound barrier at just about 700 miles per hour; today a spacecraft moves at 25,000 miles per hour.

In 1920 the most lethal instrument of destruction was the bomb or machine gun that could kill a few hundred if aimed at a cohesive human target; in 1945 two hundred thousand people died at Hiroshima from a primitive atom bomb; today up to eight million people could be killed outright and millions more injured by radiation if a single hydrogen bomb landed in the middle of London, New York or Tokyo.

In 1920 the fastest calculations were made on a mechanical adding machine. Even in 1945 there were no computers in use; by 1970 the latest generation of computers could perform a million calculations a second.

In 1920 radio was in its infancy; in 1945 there were only 60,000 television sets in use in Britain and no international links for it; in the summer of 1969 1,000 million people world-wide saw and heard Neil Armstrong step down the ladder on to the surface of the moon.

This is the scale of power the world is now attempting to cope with, using institutions that were largely devised before this power reached its present level. In this country our parliamentary, political party, civil service, trade union, educational and legal systems, all of them now under stress, were developed at a time when the machine capability was infinitesimal compared with what it is today. Many of our problems stem from institutional obsolescence. We live at a time in history when both the personal and collective material options open to us, and the expectations we have, are far greater than ever before. Yet a large number of people feel that they have progressively less say over the events that shape their lives, because the system, however it is defined, is too strong for them.

Many of the social tensions in Britain which we are now struggling to resolve actually derive from this feeling of waning influence. It is impossible to believe that the only liberation required can be achieved, as Conservatives suggest, by freeing a few thousand entrepreneurs from some government interference and providing them with higher material incentives by cutting personal levels of taxation. Nor can public ownership, economic planning and improved and more egalitarian social services, essential as all these are in providing the basis for further advance, alone provide the answer. There must be further fundamental changes to liberate people and allow them to lead fuller and more satisfying lives.

The process of re-equipping the human race with an entirely new set of tools, for that is what has happened, has produced two trends: the one towards interdependence, complexity and centralisation requiring infinitely greater skills in the management of large systems than we have so far been able to achieve; the other, going on simultaneously, and for the same reasons, towards greater decentralisation and human independence, requiring us to look again at the role of the individual, the new citizen, and his place in the community.

In sketching the changing relationship in democratic politics, of the huge new organisations on the one hand and the new citizen on the other, both created by technology, there is a common thread of argument. It is this. Authoritarianism in politics or industry just doesn't work any more. Governments can no longer control either the organisations or the people by using the old methods. The fact that in a democracy political authority derives from the consent of the electorate expressed at an election instead of by inheritance, as in a feudal monarchy, or through a coup d'etat, as in a dictatorship, makes practically no difference to the acceptability of authoritarianism. Except in a clear local or national emergency when a consensus may develop in favour of an authoritarian act of state, or if imposed it is accepted, big organisations, whether publicly or privately owned, and people, whoever they are, expect genuine consultation before decisions are taken that affect them.

It is arguable that what has really happened has amounted to such a breakdown in the social contract, upon which parliamentary democracy by universal suffrage was based, that that contract now needs to be renegotiated on a basis that shares power much more widely, before it can win general assent again.

Perhaps the hardest thing for politicians to understand is that government no longer rotates entirely around Parliament and the old cycle of inner-party policy formulation—intense electoral propaganda, voters' mandate and legislative implementation—important as they are. Winning an election without winning the argument may well frustrate at least a part of your purpose; and conversely winning an argument may be sufficient to solve certain problems by creating an atmosphere favourable to the achievement of your objectives. This is because most democratic countries, including Britain, are what they are because of the structure of values of those who live in them and are not just monuments to the skill of the statesmen who have governed them, or the legislation that has been enacted. Anyone aspiring to political leadership who really wishes to shape the society in which he lives has now got to devote a part, and probably a majority, of his time and skill and effort to persuading people, and listening in return to what is said to him.

Modern democracy requires a revitalisation and reformulation of the philosophy of government enshrined in the idea of Parliament. Indeed unless we can develop such a framework we will never succeed in reconciling the twin realities of the age in which we live—on the one hand the need for supremely good national and international management of complex systems and on the other hand the need to see to it that the new citizen, who is also a potential beneficiary of much new power, is able to direct and control more effectively the uses to which technology is put.

The alternative philosophy of government, now emerging everywhere on the Right, takes as the starting point of its analysis the argument that modern society depends on good management and that the cost of breakdowns in the system is so great that they really cannot be tolerated and that legislation to enforce greater and more effective discipline must now take priority over other issues. The new citizen is to be won over to an acceptance of this by promising him greater freedom from government, just as big business is to be promised lower taxes and less intervention and thus to be retained as a rich and powerful ally. But this new freedom to be enjoyed by big business means that it can then control the new citizen at the very same time that government reduces its protection for him.

A Socialist, by contrast, should never forget that he is in office in a representative capacity, regarding government as the people's instrument for shaping their own destiny. He must remember that the government is entrusted with the management, through information and communication, of the nation's affairs. Legislation may confirm a victory in argument already won; it may occasionally be used to educate, more often to protect, regulate or organise, but only as a last resort to enforce settlements that cannot be reached in any other way. The first priority is, therefore, to develop a system of government which is seen to be conducting itself openly, honestly and taking account of the views of the people it was elected to serve.

The Case for Open Government

The dangers of secrecy were vividly demonstrated by the experience of the 1929–31 Labour Government during the crisis that led to its downfall. The minutes of those Cabinets are now available, published in 1976 — when the then Labour Government was discussing plans for a new loan from the International Monetary Fund.[1]

The publication of these minutes offers an opportunity to study in detail the circumstances that led up to Ramsay MacDonald's betrayal and his formation of a National Government which then called a general election which threw Labour into opposition for nearly fourteen years. The Cabinet minutes, together with top secret Treasury memoranda and an account of the negotiations held with the Bank of England, the Tory and Liberal opposition leaders and the Wall Street bankers, throw a most important light on the true nature of British politics and international capitalism in the great economic crisis of fifty years ago.

At the very beginning of the first meeting Ramsay MacDonald stressed 'the vital importance in the national interest, of safeguarding secrecy of the facts and figures disclosed to the Cabinet'. Thus the Labour Movement was effectively excluded from any real influence until it was too late. The TUC were only given an outline of what was happening – their opposition to the cuts in benefits proposed together with their general views were dismissed as being based on 'no real appreciation of the seriousness of the situation'. The National Executive Committee of the Labour Party 'agreed to leave the whole question with the Government'.

By contrast the Tory leader Stanley Baldwin, the Liberal leader Sir Herbert Samuel and the bankers of London, New York and Paris were kept fully in touch and as a result exercised a far greater influence than the Labour Movement. What they wanted was cuts in benefits to make the working class pay for the crisis.

Since so many of the Tory and press attacks made upon the Labour Party and trade unions focus on the charge that they are 'extra-parliamentary' centres of power it is interesting to read the way in which the 'extra-parliamentary' power of the international bankers, working hand in hand with the Tory opposition, tried to impose their will on a Labour Cabinet and drove it from office.

It is not hard to understand why the establishment in 1931 wished to keep all these matters so secret. For if the Labour Movement had known in time what was happening it could have brought its influence to bear – and might have saved the day. But at least these minutes and papers can be read and studied and the necessary lessons learned from them.

At the time of the 1976 crisis we were determined to stick together and sustain the Labour Government in power because the 1931 split totally weakened the movement and left the British people to be frightened into voting for Tory policies. But we must also learn the other lesson which these minutes teach. A Labour Government can only resist the pressures put upon it by those, at home and abroad, who want to see it destroyed if it takes the movement and the people into its confidence and consults it fully before irrevocable decisions are made.

The demand for openness is a clear sign of democratic

pressure. Throughout history this demand has had to be acknowledged, albeit partially and bit by bit, by those with power in order to gain consent for the exercise of their power. Successive kings were forced by this means to concede knowledge first to the feudal barons, and then to the gentry, the merchants, and later still to the entrepreneurs in order to stave off the revolts against their power. 'Grievance before supply' — the right to be heard became an instrument for accountability to force the king to disclose his policy in order to win the support of his people. Later the struggle to secure the admission of the press to the House of Commons and bring about the publication of *Hansard* reflected the demand of the voters to know what their MPs were doing in their name. Similarly the campaign for the franchise was accompanied by the demand for knowledge. As early as 1649 the Levellers were arguing that 'common people have been kept under blindness and ignorance, and have remained servants and slaves to the nobility and the gentry. But God hath now opened their eyes and discovered unto them their christian liberty.'

'Open the books' has long been a demand of unions and employees. The whole range of government and industrial policies, especially in areas of high technology, has been the focus of the greatest campaigns for disclosure. The development of parliamentary democracy, universal education and the growth of the mass media have all increased the range of public understanding by the dissemination of knowledge about government, science and industry and have, in their turn, both reinforced democracy and stimulated pressure for disclosure. But it would be wrong to look at only one side of the balance sheet. For what also has to be considered is the growth of industrial, financial and public power which have all developed practices of secrecy, effectively keeping millions of people in ignorance of the biggest decisions which rule their lives.

This is the background against which the arguments for secrecy made by those with power have to be examined. These arguments are of various kinds, each of them understandable, but taken together they constitute an entrenchment of secrecy at a level which is becoming increasingly unacceptable.

First, there is the security case which runs like this: every

country is vulnerable to external attack and internal subversion, therefore its defence requires it to prepare plans against
these possibilities and these preparations must be kept behind
the tightest veil of secrecy. The logic of this argument is, on
the face of it, unanswerable and few will challenge it. To disclose defence secrets or internal security arrangements would be
to invite those against whom we wish to be protected to find
ways to evade the defences that otherwise they would have to
meet. No Freedom of Information legislation proposed has ever
been framed to include open access to security information.

But having said that, limits of security have to be carefully
defined to avoid a situation in which any, and every, action by
government is justified by reference to security. Every tyrant
and dictator in history has always found that an appeal to
security is the simplest way to win public acquiescence for his
tyranny or dictatorship. And today the identification of
'enemies' at home, and abroad, is still the easiest justification
for all sorts of actions that may limit civil liberties. The denial
of human rights all over the world including South Africa,
Iran, Chile, China or the Soviet Union is almost invariably
justified in this way. But we all know that strong armed forces
built up to resist foreign aggression may then be used to commit aggression abroad, or be diverted to suppress discontent
arising from legitimate demands for human rights at home.
Similarly an internal security apparatus may be established in
the guise of defending a free society and then become an instrument for eroding freedom in the society it is intended to defend.
All these distortions of security can themselves be concealed
behind the very veil of secrecy which the needs of security are
supposed to justify.

For example, total secrecy surrounded the preparations of
the Anglo-French invasion plans for Egypt in 1956; the USA-
supported attack on Cuba at the Bay of Pigs in 1961; and the
Soviet invasion of Czechoslovakia in 1968. Whatever the
military case for preserving this secrecy in advance of an immediate military operation, the real issues were always political,
and related to the policies which led up to the situation in
which Britain and France came to attack Egypt, America
came to attack Cuba or Russia came to invade Czechoslovakia.

The proper public discussion of these critical policy issues was of course prevented by the same secrecy and was later justified by the need to protect the troops just about to go into action. Foreign policy choices cannot be excluded from proper public discussion on the grounds that they involve military security. For to do so would be to make foreign policy an instrument of the military, instead of military policy being the instrument of foreign policy, which it must be in a democratic society. Any demand to extend military secrecy to cover foreign policy must be resisted.

Exactly similar limits must be placed on the extent of legitimate secrecy in matters of internal security. Obviously the publication of plans to arrest a foreign spy or a domestic terrorist would frustrate the purpose of the operation and no one in their senses would advocate doing so. But it is obviously important to draw a clear distinction between a spy and a critic; and between a terrorist and a dissident. If no such distinction is drawn the apparatus used to safeguard freedom can be used to suppress it. In countries which do not aspire to political liberty this presents no problem because the government is openly committed to the proposition that its own survival is in the interests of the people, and anyone who opposes the government is therefore an enemy of the people. But in societies which allow the people freely to decide who is to form the government no such argument can be sustained. Indeed in such democratic societies the freedom of the people so to decide is the test by which freedom is judged—not the survival of the government. In such societies the decision by the people as to whether they wish the government to be replaced depends upon a free and an unfettered debate between supporters of the government and its critics and other dissidents. There is always the risk that internal security measures, introduced to defend freedom, could be abused under the veil of the secrecy justified to deal with spies and terrorists to harass critics and dissidents and if this were to happen it could destroy the very freedom these measures are intended to defend.

The balance between freedom and security poses special difficulty in political democracies and requires wider public debate. First, it should be obvious that while the specific measures adopted for internal security may need to be protected, the policy, overall extent and methods of the security services are legitimate subjects for public discussion and decision together with the sums of money spent upon them. These are domestic policy issues comparable to the foreign policy issues which should dictate the defence policy of the nation. And if we are to insist that the internal security services are to be under democratic control then the policy they follow must be the subject of full public debate in the light of adequate information. In dictatorships of right or left such a proposition would not be entertained for a moment. But in democratic societies the issues are real and immediate. They require our attention because national security is still the major argument used for absolute secrecy covering foreign and defence policy and domestic police powers. Unless we can think through these difficult issues we could find that the term 'national security' becomes a blanket excuse for secrecy on any matter which the government of the day wishes to exclude from public scrutiny.

In Britain defence secrets are guarded by the Official Secrets Act. Foreign policy is more widely discussed but is still subject to the protection of government position papers, diplomatic exchanges and negotiating briefs. As far as domestic security is concerned normal police activities are discussed, but the operations, policy and extent of the security services are completely blanked out by tight secrecy.

Only the Prime Minister is entitled to know the full extent of the operation of the security services. The only Prime Minister who has written about these matters in recent years is Harold Wilson, who devoted one chapter of his book *The Governance of Britain*. This whole chapter, only 210 words long, being the only authoritative report ever written by the only office holder able to know, merits extensive quotation:[2]

> The Prime Minister has the ultimate responsibility for the National Security Authority at home and abroad, though the home and overseas organisations concerned come departmentally under the Home Office and the Foreign and Commonwealth Office responsibility.
>
> The Number 10 responsibility is exercised through the

Secretary of the Cabinet, who is the Prime Minister's link with the authorities concerned.

The Cabinet Office account for the Secret Service vote which is published under the heading '*Other external relations: Secret Service* being the *Estimate* of the amount required in the year ending ... '

In 1975/6 it amounted to £22 million. No other details of estimates or expenditure are made available to Parliament either in the estimates or the accounts. By agreement of the Public Accounts Committee the account is supported by the personal certificate of the Comptroller General in a unique form: 'I certify, that the amount shown in this account to have been expended, is supported by certificates from the responsible Ministers of the Crown'.

The Prime Minister is occasionally questioned on matters arising out of his responsibilities. His answers may be regarded as uniformly uninformative.

There is no further information that can usefully or properly be added before bringing this chapter to an end.

Against that background of officially supported public ignorance it is necessary to turn to the United States of America to find any serious public discussion about these matters. It is greatly to the credit of the Americans that faced with a clear abuse of power by the executive, they were determined to bring all these issues out into the open. Apart from the direct investigation into the Watergate Affair, a proper inquiry was held into the conduct of the security services by Senator Church, and it brought to light information about matters which in Britain would never have been disclosed.

The following is a passage from a speech made on the subject by a member of the Church Committee — the then Senator Walter Mondale, who would soon become the Vice-President of the United States, and whose words acquire their importance by virtue both of his intimate knowledge of the investigative committee of which he was a member, and his high position in the American Government.

He said:

Our investigation showed that many of the abuses of the Nixon years could be traced back to the attitudes of the Cold War. Fastened on us was the fearful myth that America could not be defended without more deceit and illegality than democracy permits — and without more cynicism and hypocrisy than our beliefs would allow. For years, the assumption was used to justify actions abroad — from subversion of freely elected governments, to assassination attempts aimed at foreign leaders. And inevitably, in Macbeth's words, the invention returned home 'to plague the inventor'.

The CIA came home to launch 'operation chaos' — a surveillance programme directed against American citizens — even though that agency is forbidden from exercising internal security functions. The law didn't matter.

The army spied on the lawful democratic activities of groups ranging across the political spectrum — from Carl McIntyre's Conservative Christian Action Movement and the John Birch Society to the Urban Coalition, the anti-defamation league, and even the Chamber of Commerce. The law didn't matter.

There was massive invasion of privacy. For years the FBI and the CIA illegally tapped phones and engaged in other forms of electronic surveillance. The law didn't matter.

The FBI and CIA both opened the private mail of American citizens. Over 300,000 first class letters were opened — mail of people like John Steinbeck, Senators Church and Kennedy, and organisations like the Federation of American Scientists. The law didn't matter.

The National Security Agency obtained from major international cable companies copies of all private telegrams sent overseas by American citizens in businesses. The law didn't matter.

Legitimate law enforcement functions were twisted and perverted. In 1969 the Internal Revenue Service established a

'Special Services Staff' to examine the tax returns of individuals—not because they had violated the tax laws, but because some people in government did not like their politics. The law didn't matter.

Eventually these agencies resorted to the commission of common crimes to obtain what they considered necessary information. So the FBI and the CIA illegally broke into the homes and businesses of American citizens—the so-called 'black bag jobs'. They even established official liaison with organised crime. The law didn't matter.

Perhaps the most terrifying abuse of power during this period was what the FBI called Cointelpro. That ugly little acronym would have been at home in any police state in Eastern Europe or Latin America. It meant illegal investigations targeted against American law abiding individuals in groups and punishment administered not by a court but by a government agency—through harassment and tactics designed to break up marriages, destroy reputations, terminate employment, sabotage political campaigns and even encourage violent retribution by falsely and anonymously labelling intended victims as government informers.[3]

The United States has now made a serious effort to open up a discussion on the proper limits of security in a democratic society. There has of course been a long tradition in the United States Congress of committees and committee hearings at which members of the executive have been required to answer questions that in Britain we would never be allowed to ask. Now there is a Freedom of Information Act which has conferred a right to know on citizens.

There are many people in Britain who would like to see the same openness here; and who cannot, in the absence of information, assess whether or not abuses of a comparable kind could occur here. Maybe the ultimate authority of the Prime Minister is effective in preventing it—but Harold Wilson said the public is not entitled to know more than he disclosed in his chapter.

I have dwelt on security at great length for obvious reasons. First, that political freedom must be secured. Second, that true security for that purpose must require secrecy. Third, that the border line between legitimate secrecy, and the abuse of power in the name of security, is one that must be defined to prevent it justifying total secrecy.

Another argument for secrecy that is most commonly advanced is based upon the maintenance of financial and commercial interests. The main advocates of secrecy on these grounds are of course those whose own interests are involved. Banks are extremely secretive about their policy and practices; so are major business firms, and the decision-making of multi-nationals and international financial institutions is shrouded in such mystery that even governments do not find it easy to discover what is really going on.

Pressure for full disclosure is likely to be met by a blank refusal accompanied by due warnings of the consequences if disclosure were to be forced. There is no doubt that the publication, in advance, of details of specific negotiations by industrial or banking enterprises could frustrate the objectives the negotiations were intended to secure. Governments may be in a similar position. But having identified those narrow categories of information where the requirements of secrecy are strictly limited in terms of time, the rest could easily be released without damage to the organisation concerned. Indeed, without information, it is impossible for the *policy* that lies behind the decisions to be properly discussed; and for the people who make these policy decisions to be held accountable for what they have done.

A third defence of secrecy is that the records about individuals relating to their own personal affairs should be protected from publication. Since such records are of no interest in terms of public policy there is no pressure to include such categories of information within the scope of any Freedom of Information policy. Indeed the argument works the other way. There is growing anxiety in many parts of the world that information may be accumulated about individuals for one purpose, and then grouped together in centralised computer records that could be used for purposes other than that for which the information was gathered. In plain English there is a fear that dossiers may be collected which, if kept secret from the person to whom they relate, could infringe his or her liberty by making it easier for him or her to be penalised, harassed or in some way disadvantaged. It is also possible for mistakes to be made and it is theoretically possible for untrue statements to be included in such records for malicious reasons. In this situation the only real safeguard is to confer a right upon all persons to know what is on their own files, so that they can correct errors, challenge unfair judgments and 'clear their names' literally. Such a remedy requires personal disclosure but not publication. We have not yet achieved that right.

Apart from these three arguments relating to military, financial and personal information which may need to be protected—and all of which require secrecy limited to the extent which is necessary, a whole host of other arguments are advanced for maintaining secrecy over a far wider range of subjects. These arguments need to be listed in order to reveal the extent of the opposition to openness that still persists in official quarters.

It may be said that the issues are too complicated for the lay public to understand; that the public are not really interested; that wide consultation will be costly and cause delay; or make administration more difficult; or that discussions will narrow the government's freedom of manoeuvre; or weaken its negotiating stance; or subject it to unhelpful external pressures; and sometimes that the publication of information collected by government would destroy the confidence of those who gave that information and inhibit people from speaking their mind. But if all these arguments fail to carry weight it may be asserted that the government has a duty to govern and that disclosure erodes the power necessary to do that duty.

In the course of my life as a minister I have heard all these arguments used many times over and, in some shape or form, they constitute the real reason why open government is so strongly resisted. It is that disclosure weakens the prerogative of ministers and the role of officials who enjoy their greatest power when they alone know what is up for decision, what the choices are and what are the relevant facts. Then their advice is hard to challenge. Seen from an official or ministerial view-point these are obviously attractive arguments. But to accept them would be to accept that the convenience of the govern-ment is synonymous with the national interest; and that the national interest actually requires the exclusion of the public from enjoying any real role in formulating policy, or exercising any effective influence before decisions are made.

How Secrecy Is Maintained at Present

If these, then, are the arguments for secrecy that predominate in large organisations and especially within government, how is it sustained?

Various techniques are used. Firstly, there is the *Official Secrets Act*. This legislation covers everything from espionage designed to undermine the security of the state, to the protec-tion of all official documents covering the whole range of government work. The workings of the Official Secrets Act have recently been the subject of a great deal of public discus-sion and inquiry, and the government have recently published a White Paper proposing changes in Section 2 of the Act and indicating a readiness to consider some proposals for wider reform. However, at the time of writing, it is an offence in law to disclose any documents or information acquired in the con-duct of official duties.

The proponents of reform fall into two categories. There are first those who want to confer the statutory right to know subject to safeguards kept to a necessary minimum; and second there are those who want to make the minimum number of changes designed to stave off the pressure for real reform — leaving us with official secrets legislation that, unlike the present Act, would command sufficient public and judicial support to make prosecutions possible.

This latter school of thought, which is strongly held by the Establishment, inside and outside the government, is also prepared to accept the need for greater disclosure of informa-tion than hitherto — so long as the decision as to whether, and what, to publish is strictly controlled by the executive as part of its prerogative. What this school of thought will not have is the entrenchment of the statutory right to know that would pass the initiative to the citizen.

But it would be a mistake to regard the Official Secrets Act as being the sole, or even the prime, instrument by which secrecy is observed. There are in fact a number of equally important techniques and institutional arrangements which reinforce it. Of these, the protection of public records under the *Thirty Year Rule* merits separate consideration.

Under this rule more than a generation has to elapse before the citizens are allowed to know the thinking that lay behind even the most major government decisions which affected their lives. The justification for this rule rests mainly on the argument that the knowledge that minutes and papers and records of discussions might be published in less than thirty years would inhibit the candid expression of opinion by ministers and officials and thus endanger the free exchange of views which good government requires. These arguments are different from the arguments for protecting current discussions, the immediate secrecy necessary for diplomatic and other negotiations, or budgetary preparations. It is in fact an argument that is based on the *principle* that accountability by publication is incompatible with good government and hence that democracy which depends upon accountability must be limited by a time gap of thirty years. Democracy can be properly described as the institutionalisation of a process by which society can learn from its own experience—and especially by its own mistakes. This being so, a thirty-year time gap before that experience and those mistakes can be published in full must necessarily mean that the learning process is at best ineffective and at worst almost useless.

In this context attempts to restrict the right of ministers to publish their own experience has to be seen as especially relevant. This policy—in so far as it is effective—is intended to prohibit those citizens elected to serve in high office from conveying their experience to those who elected them, unless the Cabinet Office have approved the text. Anthony Nutting, Dick Crossman, Selwyn Lloyd and others almost certainly committed technical breaches of the conventions in publishing what they did about events that occurred less than thirty years before the books they wrote were published.

A third restriction on open government is the *Privy Councillor's Oath*. All Cabinet ministers are, upon appointment, sworn into the Privy Council by an oath administered in the presence of the Sovereign. This oath, which has now been published, imposes a special duty upon all ministers to preserve the secrecy of government and Cabinet business to which they become privy. It is a powerful reinforcement of the Official Secrets Act in relation to ministers.

Fourthly, there is the constitutional convention of *collective Cabinet responsibility* which is thought to be central to the workings of the British constitution and has considerable implications for the secrecy of government.[4] Under this doctrine the myth of Cabinet unity on all matters discussed is fostered. Cabinets are of course rarely united in their views. Indeed were they so there would be no Cabinet discussion at all.

Why then is this myth fostered? In its origins it was a protection for the sovereign's principal advisers, against attempts by the sovereign to pick out those ministers who were ringleaders in promoting advice unacceptable to the crown. It must simultaneously have been clear that Parliament and the populace could best be kept quiescent if they were told that the Cabinet was solidly behind every policy announced by HMG; and thus dissatisfied groups could not nourish the hope of a change of policy based on the knowledge that their view was being advocated in the highest councils of the state. Later as the franchise extended the democratic influences, party unity became a major factor in securing electoral success. This too gave a practical reinforcement to the idea of collective Cabinet responsibility.

It is certainly both right and necessary that Cabinet colleagues should meet to discuss the options before them, and should agree to stick together in defending the choice made. Common sense and ordinary personal loyalty must require defeated minorities to accept the majority decision and to explain and defend it. But there is no reason whatsoever why this necessary and sensible principle should be extended to the necessarily false pretence that no alternative policies were considered, no real debate took place, and that everyone present was convinced of the merits of the majority view — as distinct from accepting that it was the majority view and that as such it should be supported. The narrow interpretation of collective Cabinet responsibility denies citizens essential knowledge of the processes by which their government reaches its decisions.

In addition to these factors working for secrecy there is the effect of patronage in enforcing it. In this context the Prime Minister's powers to hire and fire ministers without a requirement to consult, or seek parliamentary approval of any kind, for either process can naturally be used to enforce secrecy.

Harold Wilson, who formed four separate administrations over an eight-year period, appointed or reshuffled 100 Cabinet ministers and 403 ministers of state and junior ministers, created 243 peers, appointed 24 chairmen of nationalised industries controlling 20 per cent of the nation's gross production and 16 chairmen of Royal Commissions to administer various policies or make recommendations for future policy, controlled all top line appointments within the Civil Service and, of course, the Honours List.[5] For not one of these appointments is a Prime Minister constitutionally required to consult Cabinet, Parliament, public or party. The Premiership in Britain today is, in effect, an elected monarchy. No medieval monarch in the whole of British history ever had such power as every modern British Prime Minister has in his or her hands. Nor does any American President have power approaching this. Congress would not permit it.

There are no weapons so effective in securing compliance as the hint of possible preferment or possible dismissal which the Prime Minister of the day has in unfettered hands. All who hold ministerial office do so at the Prime Minister's pleasure. This being so, his or her view of what it is right to disclose or withhold is more likely to prevail than a minister's assessment of what it is in the public interest to publish. A system of elected ministers would produce a very different result.

There are many other techniques open to any large organisation which can have the effect of protecting information from 'unwelcome' public interest. Vice-President Mondale referred to the more extreme abuses, but private pressure, deliberate mystification, the misrepresentation of criticism and news management have all been practised to a greater or lesser degree by all those who have held power in all countries throughout the whole of human history. These, then, are some of the means by which secrecy is maintained. But it would of course be entirely wrong to conclude that the blanket on official information is in any sense effective — or is even intended to be effective. For the practices followed differ substantially from what the formal position suggests. A brief reference to these practices is therefore in order.

Leaks and How They Occur

Although much official information is withheld a great deal of it is officially released. The mass of White Papers, government publications, official statements of statistics and reports of commissions, working parties and committees constitutes a fair volume of output. There are ministerial speeches in Parliament and outside, press releases and press conferences and articles and broadcasts on radio and television. The volume of official publications has steadily increased. Ministers are, by long-established convention, permitted to release information which they believe it to be in the public interest to release.

In parallel with all this goes an equally well-established practice of ministers and officials giving unofficial background briefings to journalists—including the lobby. These non-attributable briefings at No. 10, or the House of Commons or in government departments are accepted by the correspondents concerned on the basis on which they are offered—namely that sources are not identified. The government can then fly kites, offer an analysis or explanation that advances their policy, or feed out selected pieces of information. But it should be noted that such practices all leave the discretion entirely with the government and are themselves secretly conducted.

It is now well known that a great deal of information about government gets out as a result of unauthorised disclosure or 'leaks'. It is common knowledge that some ministers, officials or those who have come into the possession of information which they wish to become public knowledge have, as individuals, passed it on to journalists or others. The motive for these leaks may be to win public support for a particular policy by letting it be known that an important choice is just about to be made. A regular procedure exists for inquiring into leaks of this kind but it is rarely if ever successful in identifying the source or sources.

Much of the information that appears in the press derives from such sources and they can be as embarrassing for ministers as they are valuable for the shaping of a public understanding of government policy discussions. It is rare for official documents to leak. But two examples, one for the US and one for the UK, deserve a mention because of the motivation which lay behind them. The most famous and the most recent was the deliberate publication of the Pentagon Papers by Daniel Ellsberg. He was so concerned by what he learned about the conduct of the Vietnam war by the US administration that he resolved deliberately to make the facts known to help the anti-war campaign. For Ellsberg it was a matter of conscience and in defence as he saw it of the American national interest. The other case occurred in this country during the 1930s although the facts only came to light quite recently in the *Daily Telegraph*,[6] under the headline 'Whitehall Spies Fed Churchill Secrets in 1930's':

> Sir Winston Churchill received hundreds of secret documents surreptitiously removed from official files, sent to him in breach of the Official Secrets Act when he was fighting appeasement as a back bench MP. Mr Martin Gilbert, Sir Winston's biographer, reported that these documents had been found at the Churchill Archives at Chartwell and said 'there was total, consistent and persistent breach of the Official Secrets Act' ...

Presumably those officials or serving officers who abstracted these documents and sent them to Mr Churchill were moved by the same motives as Daniel Ellsberg — namely a concern for the British national interest and a fear that interest was being betrayed by the then government.

This, then, is the balance sheet as best as I can draw it up at the moment.

The growing demand for open government is still being held back by the sort of arguments set out above, while the present practices succeed in restricting disclosure to the prerogative of the executive, supplemented by briefings. Meanwhile evasions of the law and custom are growing, have been to some extent accepted, and few if any of them can be held to have inflicted serious damage on the national interest though governments may have been embarrassed for a time. But the question is not whether there are sufficient breaches of secrecy to satisfy the idle curiosity of the public or to furnish material for commentators to write their articles in the press. The real issue is whether the public interest is served by the present system as it is supposed to work. The answer must be 'no'. For when we discuss the subject, it is not an arid constitutional technicality that we are considering but the central question of the method by which current decisions are made which affect the lives of all of us, and determine the deployment of massive financial resources and resources of highly skilled people.

If we accept that the control of information about those decisions and how they are arrived at is a prerogative of government, then we are also accepting that democracy cannot become mature enough to allow the people to share even the thinking that precedes those decisions. The extent to which governments should become open cannot be left to the discretion of ministers alone. It should be entrenched in a statutory right to know which transfers the prerogative for initiating demands for disclosure to citizens and then Parliament. At the same time there must be absolute safeguards for information bearing on genuine questions of national security and protection for citizens with regard to information concerning them.

Any serious attempt to secure real democratic control would require some major changes:

First, a series of Select Committees should be established. They should cover the work of each department with an effective power to see all relevant papers — save for the narrow range of real security-classified documents already mentioned. These committees should include ones on the following subjects:

   i Economic policy
  ii Industrial policy
 iii Foreign affairs
 iv Defence policy
  v Agriculture
 vi Machinery of government.

Such committees should have the power to call for briefs from the departments concerned setting out alternative strategies and to call before them any minister or senior official for cross-examination where possible before decisions are made, but in all cases after they have been announced. They should be provided with proper staff and facilities and should be free, if they think it right, to hold their hearings in public and with the press present.

More open government has long been hinted at by ministers in all parties as an indication of their sympathy for greater public participation in political decisions. But very little indeed has been done to bring it about.[7] Secrecy in decision-making does not occur by accident or by default. It is because knowledge is power and no government willingly gives up power to the Commons, the public, or anyone else. Open government would disclose more about the processes of decision-making including the workings of the Cabinet committee system, reveal the role of officials and advisers and involve both admitting and encouraging pressures upon ministers.

Hansard is honoured in our history because of the battles that preceded the right of press and public to read what was actually being said in the Commons chamber. Undoubtedly the next stage in this struggle for publication is set to begin. Why should Cabinet papers be locked up for thirty years before the public may see them? If parliamentary democracy is—as I believe—a unique system of government partly because it allows us to learn from our own mistakes in time to correct them, the raw material of that experience must be made available in time to use it for that purpose. It is not as if attempts to impose secrecy are effective. We all know that they are not.

Political correspondents explain—as best they can—what is

going on in Whitehall and Downing Street. But since the authorised versions of events are so selective, the public gets the gossip without the texts, and this necessarily obscures instead of clarifying the great issues of public policy that are under discussion.

More openness is especially necessary now that all major political parties are coming to be seen and understood for what they are — broad coalitions embracing different tendencies within them. Everybody knows that the Labour Party, the Labour conference, the National Executive and the parliamentary Labour Party contain people with many different views, some loosely linked into groups with their own leaders, supported by their own publications. In recent years a much greater acceptance of all these tendencies has developed within the party. We have, in my opinion, benefited greatly from this new maturity and toleration and I hope and believe that we shall never revert to the intolerant practices of the past whether against groups on the left or groups on the right.

Some of these tendencies are reflected within the Cabinet itself. The Manifesto group is there represented, and so is the Tribune group. Those who, like myself, have never been a member of either group would not want to see it otherwise.

It was a Labour Government which invented the important constitutional doctrine of 'dissenting ministers' during the referendum on the EEC and thus publicly admitted the obvious fact that no Cabinet is ever always unanimous on everything. Collective Cabinet responsibility under which all ministers describe, explain and defend majority Cabinet decisions no longer extends to the maintenance of the fiction that members of Cabinet minorities all experience an immediate conversion to the majority view at the very moment when the Prime Minister records it in his summing up. In my opinion this recent recognition of an old reality is deeply reassuring and not, as is sometimes argued, a sign of the imminent collapse of democratic government. If Parliament, public and press have now braced themselves to accept the plain and obvious truth that Cabinet discussions are interesting, vigorous and sometimes revolve around alternative policies, why should even the disclosure of an outline of the points at issue — while these discussions are in progress—be guarded, so relentlessly and so ineffectively, from any risk of publicity? No newspaper account or 'think piece' in the weeklies or even a television reconstruction of a Cabinet discussion is a satisfactory substitute for the right of Parliament and public to know what the major choices are before certain important decisions are made. Censorship and rumour feed on each other and it would be in the public interest to dispense with both.

The House of Commons should—on major issues which permit it—insist on its right, directly or through Select Committees, to get the facts, see the papers, question the ministers and their officials wherever possible before the Cabinet reaches its view. No system of this kind will be easy or perfect. But unless the Commons boldly claims on behalf of the electorate greater knowledge of what is happening it will slowly shrink back to the role of ex-post-facto auditor of decisions already taken, leaving government MPs with nothing to do but troop through the lobbies in endless votes of confidence that merely rubber-stamp government decisions which they did not shape because they did not know the facts in time to do so.

Second, the House of Commons must restore its control over major public appointments made under its prerogative. One of the greatest achievements of parliamentary democracy in the past was the victory the Commons secured over the monarchy in the choice of ministers of the crown. Her Majesty's ministers since then have served not at the pleasure of the sovereign but only for so long as they enjoyed the confidence of a majority of members of the House of Commons. Most of the royal prerogatives of the past are now exercises on ministerial advice for which the administration is answerable to Parliament. But in recent years a mass of new patronage based on the royal prerogative has grown up which is dispensed by ministers without Commons control. I am not now referring to the appointment of archbishops, bishops and judges, which have historically been at the disposal of the Prime Minister. I am referring to the thousands of appointments to public office for which there is no constitutional requirement for parliamentary approval.

We have already discussed the public sector of industry which employs a million and three-quarter workers, has a gross turnover of £14 billion a year and produces 20 per cent of our national output. Since 1949, 85 chairmen of the nationalised industries have been appointed by successive Prime Ministers without any constitutional requirement to consult anyone.[8] Not one of these chairmen has been submitted for public examination by the House of Commons or its Select Committees under the sort of confirmation procedures which the American Congress insists upon when presidential nominations to high office are made.

Such a confirmation procedure, if adopted by our Parliament, would redress the balance immediately in favour of the legislature and the electors it serves, against ministers and the officials who serve them.

Let me take another example—this time relating to the choice of ministers themselves. As we have mentioned, the power of a Prime Minister to appoint ministers is constitutionally unfettered. Thus it is the 23 Cabinet ministers, 32 ministers of state and 52 junior ministers—well over 100 ministers in all (not to mention PPSs)—are appointed, dismissed or reshuffled without any consultation whatever with the parliamentary party on the government side of the House, whichever party is in power.

It is not so, as far as Labour is concerned, when we are in opposition. Each year the parliamentary Party elects its Parliamentary Committee or Shadow Cabinet, leaving only the allocation of shadow portfolios to the Leader of the Opposition to make. There are many Labour MPs who would argue, and I would agree with them, that nothing would do more to strengthen the influence of members of Parliament than maintaining that election system for the Cabinet when Labour is in power. But however it is done, the power of patronage now exercised by the Prime Minister and other ministers must be brought under far greater Commons control.

Third, the House of Commons must seek a mandate from the people to achieve the complete end of the House of Lords. The battle between the people and the Lords is an old one. Painfully, stage by stage, the Lords' veto was ended in 1910 and the delaying power cut again in 1948. Changes in composition have also been carried through. Now the time has come to develop the work of the Commons so that it can replace the Lords without any loss of parliamentary scrutiny.

This is not an argument based on the political balance as it exists in the House of Peers. It is because it is inherently wrong that the laws of this land should be submitted for approval to a body of men and women who lack any democratic mandate at all. It is not just that an inherited seat in Parliament is an anachronism — though it is. It is that the powers of patronage which are used by Prime Ministers to place people in Parliament by personal preferment are equally offensive. Let me illustrate my argument with figures. The 635 MPs elected to the Commons in 1974 were put there by an electorate totalling just over 40 million people. By comparison 639 peers were put in the House of Lords by the last seven Prime Ministers.[9]

It cannot be right that seven men — however distinguished — should wield the same power to make legislators as do 40 million voters. The simplest way to cut out this patronage is to end the chamber which lives on it. I believe there would be strong public support for parliamentary democracy to be strengthened in this way, and the day will come when it will be done.

Fourth, there must be a comprehensive Freedom of Information Act. This should confer upon Parliament and the electors the statutory right to information. There is no need to make a detailed case for this here since it arises naturally from all that we have so far discussed.

Fifth, the security services should be accountable to Parliament and the people. This could be done through a special House of Commons Select Committee, meeting when necessary in secret, composed exclusively of Privy Councillors. The committee should be empowered to question responsible ministers and security officers on the whole range of their policies and activities — and to report annually to Parliament in a form that can be published.

In October 1978 I proposed that the Labour Party National Executive set up an inquiry into the workings of the security services. My main reason for doing so was the increasing public concern at the possibility that the security services may be

abusing their privileged position as guardians of our democratic freedoms.[10]

Citizens must also be concerned at the possibility that,
through extensive surveillance, computerised dossiers and
secret files may have been compiled which cover a wide range
of people, beliefs and activities that extend far beyond any
possible threat to our security. Every country in the world
maintains espionage, counter-espionage services, and has a
political police force of some kind. In dictatorships these
services are intended to maintain the government in power.
But in democracies like Britain the avowed intent of the
security services is to safeguard democratic rights against
external or internal attack, and for this purpose they operate in
secret. There is, however, an obvious danger that the security
services may—just because their work is secret—drift into
practices which could actually undermine, or endanger, the
freedom they are supposed to defend. If we are to avoid this
there is a case for publishing every year all information about
these services which can be published without endangering
security.

These would perhaps include details of their budgeting and
staffing; the names of those in charge of the security services;
the guidelines issued to these services relating to their objectives
and methods; the number of dossiers in existence relating to
political activities; a report on the reasons for collecting these
dossiers and an account of what happens to the information
acquired for inclusion in them; an annual report on the total
number of interceptions of communications by phone or mail;
a full list of the foreign security services with which the UK
security services have arrangements for reciprocal exchange of
information, or with which they work.

We should consider giving citizens the same rights to
information about records and files kept on them as are enjoyed
by US citizens under contemporary US legislation. We should
also press for the introduction of a 'Security Services Annual
Act' under which, as with the Army and Air Force Annual
Acts of earlier years, Parliament gains the ultimate control of
the security services, as it did the standing army in 1689.[11]

There would, I feel, be widespread support for any serious

contribution that the Labour Party might be able to make to this problem which is causing concern to so many serious people in so many countries of the world. To the extent that we are able to make our security services accountable, those charged with the difficult and disagreeable task of protecting our freedoms might feel that their work was better understood; and thus enjoy greater public acceptance than is now the case.

Conclusion

When the history of this period comes to be studied in greater depth it may well be that Britain's present problems will be seen to stem from too little democracy and not from too much. We may come to see that the personal power vested in past Prime Ministers to the exclusion of Cabinet, Parliament, public and party has been a major factor in hindering our free and open society from resolving these problems more easily. The purpose of this section has been to set out some of the ways in which people in this country can have a far greater say in the decisions which affect their lives. I have listed above some of the practical ways in which the people and their elected representatives can gain access to the information they will need if they are to play a bigger role in the democratic government of our country. This is by no means comprehensive. There will also have to be a vast extension of industrial democracy, as discussed in Chapter 7. On top of this a genuine democracy can only function if the mass media — newspapers and television — are prepared to play their part in making available to the public a full range of ideas, opinions and information about the way our world turns.

ISSUES FOR THE
1980s

6

The Arguments

Not long ago on a train to Birmingham a youngish man with blue jeans sat opposite me and I said, 'What do you do?' He replied, 'I make fancy belts.'

'Would you show me one?'

'Yes,' he replied and he brought out a belt with a buckle.

'Do you make a living out of it?'

'I make a sort of living.'

'How long have you done it for?'

'Six months.'

'What did you do before that?' I asked.

'I was a tool-maker,' he said.

A tool-maker is one of the most highly skilled engineering craftsmen. In most of the bazaars of the Middle East they are trying to turn fancy-belt makers into tool-makers. They would give their eye-teeth for tool-makers. Yet because Britain has failed to provide the capital funds and equipment for the most highly skilled the process is going the wrong way. We are de-industrialising. As a result we are in danger of losing the economic strength needed as a basis for our welfare state.

Broadly speaking, there are three types of possible solution on offer to the crisis exemplified by turning tool-makers into fancy-belt makers. *Monetarism*, or the return to a full-blooded *laissez-faire* capitalism; *corporatism* which means the imposition of discipline from the top to underpin the present decaying mixed economy with all its inequality and injustice; and *democratic socialism*. The purpose of this book is to show the relevance of democratic socialism to the problems we face.

The one solution that no longer seems to be on offer is social democracy, the philosophy which has dominated the last thirty years or so. At the end of the war, when we were enjoying a boom created partly by the war itself and partly by the collapse of our main competitors, the social democrats concluded that Keynesian economic management alone was sufficient to permit continual growth. They believed that growth would be easier if there was just a touch of central planning and with public ownership confined to the basic industries. This, the social democrats argued, would be enough to preserve full employment and permit a steadily rising volume of public expenditure. This would have the effect of resolving the conflict of interests between capital and labour, the recognition of which is an intrinsic part of the basic socialist analysis.

Today after a succession of cuts in public spending plans, as demanded by the international financial community, and with rising unemployment, there are few people within the Labour Party still prepared to argue that the social democratic analysis offers a way forward. Today the arguments within the party and trade union movement are between a confident democratic socialist strain which enjoys majority support and a view that a Labour government in power can automatically resolve these problems by traditional means and should be uncritically obeyed by the Labour Movement. In the country as a whole the argument is between democratic socialism and the two main alternatives now on offer, monetarism and corporatism. The choice can be set out quite simply.

The Argument in Outline

1 The economic crisis which now grips the Western industrialised world is deep-seated and fundamental.

2 Monetarism cannot resolve this crisis without endangering the social fabric of political democracy itself.

3 Corporatism, or the imposition of centralised controls from the top, is equally unacceptable and unworkable.

4 Democratic socialism which combines direct public investment in industry and expanded public expenditure combined with self-management does offer a real prospect of resolving the present deadlock, and protecting personal freedom.

5 The debate about democratic socialism which is now in progress in Britain is also taking place all over the world and its appeal is so great that it will prevail over both capitalism and communism.

The Present Crisis of Unemployment

The Western industrialised world is now suffering from very serious unemployment. At the Bonn summit in July 1978 when President Carter, Prime Minister Callaghan and the other heads of state met to confer they spoke for nations in which there were 17 million men and women out of work. And present forecasts suggest that these figures could rise still further during the 1980s. Social Security payments to the jobless are more generous than they were before the Second World War. But it would be quite wrong to suppose that the waste of human ability represented by those figures is any more acceptable to those thrown on the scrap heap, or to the societies which allow this to happen, than it was in the great inter-war depressions.

Not that the price is paid by the unemployed alone. We all pay for unemployment in a host of ways. We pay for it most directly in taxation to maintain, in unemployment, those who want to work. To do this we have to divert our tax money away from other projects in health, education and housing that are urgently required to meet essential human needs. Unemployment worsens the urban crisis, both by causing more poverty and by cutting back on the resources that are needed to deal with it. Unemployment challenges women's right to work and through work to enjoy a freer life. It heightens racial and other tensions. It destroys the pride of the breadwinner in the family and shatters the high hopes of the school leaver. Unemployment breeds despair and apathy, and in time may threaten social disruption. But above all it reveals for us to see some basic and inexplicable contradictions in our economic system. Why do we in the Western world all allow families to live in sub-standard housing side by side with building workers for whom we are told there is no work? Why do we still accept overcrowded school classes and hospitals when there are unemployed teachers and nurses who cannot practise their professions? For what reason are we expected to accept the co-existence of unmet needs, unemployed people and unused financial resources? Our economic system was not ordained by God. It was created by man—and what man invented man can change.

We should not lay the blame for what has happened at the door of any individual or group of individuals. To do so would be to resort to the crude tactic of finding scapegoats and blaming everything on them. These contradictions are fundamental to the economic system under which we operate; and that system is deadlocked and log-jammed by contradictory interests that cannot be resolved without basic economic and political reforms.

Adam Smith and the Birth of Capitalism

When Adam Smith in *The Wealth of Nations* published his economic analysis he was arguing for *laissez-faire* and free enterprise. He believed that the cumbersome and corrupt apparatus of feudalism was holding back the new technologies that man had developed. For him the 'magic hand of the market' was a better guide to the deployment of resources than the diktats of kings and the fumbling decisions of courtiers and landowners who then held sway. Adam Smith was seen as a liberator in his own time. He helped release the genius of the entrepreneur in the economic sphere and matched it by demanding the political enfranchisement of the class of capitalists who were then coming into their own. Indeed in the Western world it is still widely assumed that capitalism and democracy are inextricably bound up together and that to defend democracy it is necessary to defend capitalism even though the defence of capitalism, in practice, may lead to the denial of freedom.

But with the passage of time this simple analysis ceased to describe the true situation as it developed. If there is to be competition there must necessarily be winners and losers. And the winners of industrial competitions absorbed and took over their defeated competitors so that monopolistic corporations grew, first nationally and then internationally, until now giant multinational companies bestride the world and exercise power that owes no allegiance to nation states, many of which the corporations have outgrown in power and wealth. These great corporations still protest their ideological commitment to Adam Smith while they increasingly resemble the very feudal trading corporations which Adam Smith worked so resolutely to destroy.

Labour too responded to the challenge of capitalism in a way that Adam Smith did not anticipate. Uprooted from the rural areas, poorly housed in the new industrial towns and closeted together in factories, working people found themselves at the mercy of employers and combined into trade unions to defend their interests by collective wage bargaining. Strong trade unions, because they had no other scope for influencing events, could only press their wage claims and this process inevitably reduced the inequality upon which pure capitalism depends for its success.

But the third and most important development which occurred as a result of the Industrial Revolution was the development of the franchise itself. For once every man and woman had the vote a completely new and formidable source of economic power came on to the scene. It is inherent in the philosophy of capitalism that the biggest rewards will go to the most successful. But when the poor, and the unsuccessful, are armed with the ballot paper or the voting machine, they can vote for schools and hospitals and houses for themselves and their families which, as individuals, they could not afford to pay for.

The Welfare State, the present levels of public expenditure and the taxation to sustain it, stem directly from the pressure that the ballot box brings to bear on the economy. In short, it is now becoming clear that there are fundamental conflicts of interest between *laissez-faire* economics; industrial monopolies; free trade unions and the universal adult suffrage, which cannot be reconciled without major changes in the structure of the economy. That is the log-jam that faces Western societies and it is to the problem of clearing that log-jam that we have now most urgently to turn our minds.

Lessons from the Pre-war Slump

These are not really new problems at all. In the 1930s the Western world was also crippled by the most severe recession, brought about by the same log-jam. Various remedies were tried in various countries. In Britain a National Government was formed committed to the monetarist policies imposed by the bankers. It cut back on unemployment pay and public expenditure, but its policies did not cure unemployment. In America Franklin D. Roosevelt tried a different policy. The New Deal was an early Keynesian approach employing deficit spending to finance public works and job creation schemes. But the New Deal did not bring back full employment. Hitler and Mussolini also undertook massive civil construction projects.

None of these policies was effective until the long shadow of impending war started huge arms programmes, financed by taxation, first bringing jobs to unemployed factory workers and then putting the rest of us in uniform as soldiers also on the public pay roll. These rearmament programmes, and the war itself, involved public investment and public expenditure on a massive scale. But it brought back full employment, and, in doing so, generated the wealth to pay for it. The challenge to our generation is how to get back to full employment without rearmament and war — which nowadays could only mean the destruction of the human race.

Three Remedies on Offer

It is against that background of analysis and experience that we have to examine the remedies which are on offer to help us overcome our problems. These remedies are of three kinds.

1 MONETARISM

The first is a monetarist remedy. The argument for it is simple and straightforward. It is to lift the heavy burden of taxation from industry and commerce by sharp cuts in public investment and public expenditure in the hope that financial incentives will work once more and market forces will revert to their magical role of allocating and re-allocating resources so as to optimise their use. Dr Milton Friedman, the prophet of this school of thought, has succeeded in enthusing a large number of bankers, industrialists, economists and administrators with the beautiful simplicity of this approach which has been embraced by them with all the passion of a religious conversion. After a bonfire of controls over pay and prices and trade and industry a new, a stronger economy will rise phoenix-like from the ashes and restore economic and political freedom at a stroke.

There is, however, no evidence whatsoever to suggest either that the higher unemployment monetarism will bring would reduce the power of trade union bargaining in a complex and interdependent economy; nor that those with the ballot box in their hands will deliberately use it for deflation and to widen the gap between rich and poor with all the divisive and dangerous consequences that that would entail.

2 CORPORATISM

The second remedy is corporatist in character. This school of thought also recognises the existence of the log-jam, but recoils from the social disruption which it believes monetarism would bring. Instead it calls for a disciplined society where the men at the top in government, industry, banking and the unions would sit down together and work out a common approach which it then would become the duty of each leadership group to impose by law upon its own constituency. This school of thought also has very powerful friends in high places throughout the Western world. Indeed it is true to describe it as the consensus view of the old British establishment which, for reasons of prudence rather than from any personal preference, believe it is their best recipe for survival.

However, we should be sceptical about the prospects for corporatism. Admittedly it is a tested and tried system in that modern corporatism greatly resembles the feudalism which preceded Adam Smith's revolution. The state and the economy are to be run by a new generation of barons who now occupy their modern castles in the office blocks of London and Brussels. But full-blown corporatism too is in the long run incompatible with a free society. A free people are unlikely to swallow for long the claims of the powerful to be wiser than the rest of us, especially if their conclusions are to be imposed from above, and by a strange coincidence are so clearly in the interests of those who now enjoy power.

Total corporatism to preserve the present balance of the mixed economy is no more likely to be acceptable than would be corporatism of the kind that Mussolini and Stalin each imposed to buttress their very different political philosophies. Corporatism could last for rather longer than the jungle economics of the monetarists but neither can offer any real hope of ending the slump. Indeed the danger from a failed corporatism is that it could transform itself into a dictatorship.

3 DEMOCRATIC SOCIALISM

The third solution is democratic socialism. This is very much a home-grown British product which has been slowly fashioned over the centuries. Its roots are deep in our history and have been nourished by the Bible, the teachings of Christ, the Peasants' Revolts, the Levellers, Tom Paine, the Chartists, Robert Owen, the Webbs and Bernard Shaw who were Fabians, and occasionally by Marxists, Liberals and radicals who have all contributed their analysis to our study of society. The Labour Party comprises within its ranks representatives of a wide range of opinions. We have been wise enough not to seek to impose a common socialist dogma on anyone. Indeed our socialism grew out of our experience and was not handed down from above, or received from outside. The British Labour Movement was born out of the chapels of the dissenters and the struggles of factory workers who campaigned for trade union rights, then for the parliamentary vote, then organised themselves to nominate candidates in a separate Labour Party and finally adopted an explicitly socialist approach, based upon a full commitment to a democratic system, and personal freedom.

Our argument is also based on the recognition that there is a log-jam that must be lifted. We too accept that any society requires discipline, though the discipline of the market place and the discipline imposed by the top people are both equally unattractive. We believe that the self-discipline of full democratic control offers our best hope for the future, and is the only real answer to inflation, because it confers real responsibility.

The Labour Party has worked on the basis that the investment gap must be filled by public investment, with proper public accountability and public ownership, and that only public expenditure can convert human needs into economic demands able to command resources and help restore full employment. Indeed we believe that the nation can earn its living efficiently and profitably only if there is a new balance of wealth and power in favour of working people. And to avoid corporatism creeping in as a by-product of these public initiatives we have been working for a wider and deeper accountability of power through greater democratic control by Parliament of government and of finance and industry and of the institutions of the Labour Movement itself. Parliament and MPs freely elected are the greatest safeguards for our freedom. This is clearly understood by the Labour Party and Labour MPs.

The argument between monetarism, corporatism and democratic socialism in Britain is still going on. The wartime consensus that carried us forward for a quarter of a century broke down in 1970 having absolutely failed to correct a relative economic decline that stretches way back to the nineteenth century.

Three important schools of thought are now therefore contending for public endorsement. The British people have not yet made up their minds around which school of thought they will hope to build a new consensus. The next decade will see a growth of democratic socialism against the ideas of monetarism and corporatism. Now that we have examined each of these alternative philosophies awaiting us we can look finally at some of the main issues which are likely to dominate the politics of Britain in the 1980s: jobs, the Common Market and democracy.

7

Jobs

As we approach the 1980s we can see that Britain's economy contains certain fundamental defects. These defects derive first from a basic contradiction between the requirements of a market economy which is becoming increasingly monopolised; second, from the pressure by free trade unions; and third, from the pressure of the ballot box.

As we have already acknowledged, capitalism in its early days was very 'progressive' in the sense that it released productive forces which had been held back by feudalism. Capitalism was a means by which the surplus created by manufacturing could be reinvested in industry, under an imperial structure which gave us cheap raw materials and secure markets. For a while it was very effective but as monopoly built up in industry, as trade unionism built up as a counter-force and then as the ballot box enabled the poor to by-pass the market system to gain access to health and education and schools, this conflict brought us to the present log-jam.

No amount of fine tuning will deal with the underlying problems. In economic terms these problems are two-fold: first, how do you get the nation's savings recycled back into industry; second, how do you so organise the relationship between the three parties (capital, labour and government) in such a way as to lift the deadlock and permit production to go forward?

The capitalist world economy is in very serious difficulty. The weakness of the dollar reflects the development in the United States of the same log-jam as in the United Kingdom and this is going to make America much weaker. In Germany and France and Japan what has been called by the British press 'the British disease' will turn out to be something much deeper. It will be the ageing process of capitalism in a so-called mixed economy under parliamentary democracy and it will give rise to a search for new solutions. It is very important that the British Labour Movement, united around socialist commitment, should rediscover its self-confidence.

The most dramatic event of the whole of the last decade has been the collapse of confidence of those who espouse the system under which we now live. When Labour were in office in 1964–70, industrialists and bankers spoke as if the only obstacle to a recovery of British capitalism was this dangerous left-wing government. Once we had gone everything would come right. When we came back, four years later, their morale had been destroyed. During the whole of this period the growing confidence of the Labour Movement was quite remarkable. Those qualities of responsibility and self-confidence are now to be found in the Labour Movement and on the left, not on the right. That is why, even today when the establishment don't like a Labour government, they don't know where to turn for the sort of leadership they would like and they are not sure that even if it was available it would do the trick. This underlying change has quite transformed the prospects for democratic socialism.

Unemployment could be the catalyst. If unemployment continues to rise—and the signs are that it will—there will be great pressure for structural change. We assume too early that the present level of unemployment is tolerable. That is what would undermine a rigid monetarist policy introduced by any government in the 1980s. The British people do care about unemployment. The Germans were scarred by the memory of inflation under Weimar. We were scarred by the 1930s and this would reflect itself in pressure on the government for a self-correcting mechanism. With it will come the opportunity for socialist ideas to advance yet again.

One of the most important analytical arguments that is going on at the moment is whether we put curbing inflation or cutting unemployment as the prime objective. Nobody's going to say that inflation doesn't matter and nobody's going to say unemployment doesn't matter. But there is no doubt that the

149

way in which the argument is presented and the conclusions which we draw and the solutions that we seek do have a considerable effect on whether we end up with rather higher inflation and more people in work or a zero rate of inflation and mass unemployment. There is a danger this might happen in Britain for a number of connected and important reasons. The long-term decline of our own industry, the weakness of our industrial base, supplemented by the world slump, could create a situation from which we could not recover. Even if there was a world recovery, we would have a short, fevered boom and would then collapse because we did not have the industrial base to sustain growth in Britain. As our major competitors had re-equipped more effectively they would be in a position to use the extra demand to take up their slack capacity. If at the same time we found that the balance of payments cover of the North Sea oil ran out, we would then be in a very, very serious situation. It is important we should talk about this, not in a pessimistic way, but to open it up for discussion. The narrow, limited and obsessive talk about pay policy and inflation without having this broader picture in mind could delay public understanding of the magnitude of the job to be done.

The Pension Funds

As we have seen,[1] one of our main problems is the shortage of investment in manufacturing industry. These days the bulk of potential investment funds comes not from individual rich men, but from the financial institutions such as the insurance and pension funds, who do not necessarily use the huge sums at their disposal in a manner compatible with the public interest. This is one area where there will have to be change. The trade unions have for some time been arguing that the pension funds are one area where democracy could be applied without disturbing the even flow of management and industry. These savings belong to the workers, they are their own deferred earnings. Workers want them not only as income when they retire, but to sustain and create jobs while they are at work, and so to guarantee that they will retire in a buoyant economy.

This practical as well as moral entitlement is the case for change. It has been very much resisted. In effect what the trade unions want is representation on the committees and a move towards some agreement that would permit their representative to sit alongside investment managers in the big financial institutions to see that they are used as a development fund. Of course public revenue from North Sea oil can be used to underpin that type of investment in exactly the same way as the Export Credit Guarantees Department underpins expor contracts for the benefit of domestic industry. So public funds could sustain the value of domestic investment. Making use of the National Enterprise Board and the Scottish and Welsh Development agencies, this would be a workmanlike answer to the problem of recycling our savings into our own industry.

Without this our decline will continue. We will get in a situation where our North Sea oil revenues, which cover our balance of payments, could become a mask behind which de-industrialisation takes place. Not only would we run out of oil in the end. We would have demobilised ourselves behind the very deceptive front of international solvency. That is a serious danger.

New Technology

Next we have to address ourselves to the fact that investment in new technology is labour-saving. We are in a dilemma: more investment in new technology could mean less jobs; on the other hand, if we don't re-equip, we will be so inefficient that we could face mass unemployment such as occurred in our motorbike, shipbuilding and car industries. If we do re-equip with new technology, then we are faced in a more acute form with arguments about who will control it, in whose interests will it be developed and then, even if we get that right, we have to decide how the increase in leisure time should be distributed.

Are we going to have a small group of white-collar people earning £10,000 a year, on overtime, and 60 per cent of the population living on social security and being kept back by armed guards because they would be so discontented? That is one choice. The other is more leisure.

The issue is not whether we accept or reject new technology.

The issue is how are we to distribute the benefits from the use of new technology. The benefits from the use of the tools, the labour-saving element, can be distributed in many ways. If it were possible for everybody to be at work and working a four-day month, who would complain? The puritanical idea of the moral worth of hard physical labour was invented to give capitalism its driving force in the seventeenth, eighteenth and nineteenth centuries.

One of the opportunities that modern technology opens up when fewer people are engaged in the productive process will be the release of effort for environmental improvement; coal tips have been landscaped, clean air and pollution programmes have been instituted along with funding of home insulation. All these are labour intensive, offer prospects for work and can make industrial development more environmentally acceptable.

New technology will enable us to enjoy a rising standard of living, but we must ask ourselves what constitutes rising living standards. Is it just more transistors, a new car every year, a stereo, a colour television? Or is it a conception of the quality of life that is based upon service and human relationships and the meeting of human needs which are entirely labour intensive and which don't involve the wasteful deployment of minerals? Rising living standards must involve the development of those public and social services and service industries which we now for the first time can contemplate and which are hungry for labour. You can't mechanise the curing of the sick or the teaching of children or the training of adults. The contradiction, to which socialists have often drawn attention, of unmet needs, unused resources and unemployed people side by side must be resolved. With the revenue that comes from efficient production using new technology you can convert the unmet needs into real demand by public funding, and in that way open up opportunities for new jobs.

Growth

Then we have resolved another problem, the problem of how you can have continuing growth in a world where there are limited mineral resources. Fossil fuels and raw materials are diminishing, but the one natural resource that is growing at an explosive rate is human knowledge, human skill and know-how. That know-how allows you to make use of diminishing mineral resources in a more intelligent way and to recycle them to reduce waste. Knowledge is not depletable. There is no limit to the amount of science we can learn, no limit to the amount of history we can learn, or to the extent to which we can upgrade the general level of skill. We can now begin to see a new perspective of economic and social growth with rising living standards that do not solely depend on producing new-style consumer goods every year and throwing away the old ones in a dump that wrecks somebody else's environment.

A degree of intelligent and democratic planning could supersede the concept of market forces as a magical way of distributing wealth. We have got to make the leap from the world of market forces towards more democratic decisions about resources and a greater respect for human values. The cruder the operation of market forces the more repression would be necessary to make people accept them. The more we can build on the possibilities that are opening up and on an understanding of what is possible, the more people will reject market forces. The strengthening of democratic controls will lead them towards a different sort of society.

For this to occur the trade union movement will have to develop a far wider range of demands and be prepared to assume new responsibilities. Wage militancy alone will not transform society and pursued by itself, without wider demands, can actually damage the prospects of advance. Collective bargaining must necessarily be extended to cover the whole range of company policy. At the same time government and industry will have to concede that workers have a part to play in the management of the economy which extends well beyond the right to negotiate simply about pay and immediate conditions of work.

Since the war almost every economic policy has ended up with a demand for wage restraint. This was true of Stafford Cripps; Selwyn Lloyd; Macmillan in the end; George Brown; Ted Heath; and this is how it worked out in the 1974–79 Labour Government. What was said about the role of wage policy, that if we could restrain wages we would then solve the problems of our economy, was not correct. Many efforts were made and with a great deal of goodwill. To have driven ourselves into the same cul-de-sac so many times since the war should now make us realise that there must be some defect in the argument.

It is indisputable that wages play an important part in the distribution of wealth in the economy. They also play a part (though they are not necessarily the only factor) in the level of inflation. Whether wages policy is voluntary or statutory, whether it is accompanied by a prices and incomes board or a relativities board is really secondary to the question of whether the restraint of wages is the key to the recovery of the British economy. However wages are fitted into a sensible national plan, to focus upon them alone and give undue emphasis to their role in conditioning recovery is to get it wrong. We must begin with a deep scepticism about what has been said about wages policy since the war.

It has been demonstrated that wage militancy may not lead to permanent gains.[2] This tends to confirm the view that, on both sides, arguments about wages are seen as having played too important a part in economic policy. The real question is how to get the nation's savings recycled into the nation's industry; how to get production up to employ more people; how to redistribute the benefits of full employment in a rise in real living standards. One of the reasons why wage militancy has tended to be the peg around which trade unions have concentrated is that it is the one area, indeed the only area, where trade unions have been permitted by law to be effective. If you say to the trade union movement, as we still do, 'The law does not entitle you to discuss investment, the prices of your products, research and development, export marketing, product development,' then the whole weight of trade union activity will remain concentrated on the wages side and this may not be effective in securing a real change in the balance of wealth and power in society.

What needs to be done? Both the failure of wages policy and the failure of wage militancy point to the need to examine the real causes of progressive decline. Does free collective bargaining, limited to wages, hold the key or should we look at the extension of free collective bargaining to encompass all those decisions that really determine whether there is wealth creation in society, or not? If not, then we must move towards free collective bargaining about wages, prices, investment, products, exports, manpower forecasting and product development. If we look at it this way, then by definition (because we are broadening the range of trade union functions) we are moving out of the area where wages alone become the key.

Perhaps we should add one point. The fact that there are figures which show a reduction in real living standards despite wage militancy lends credence to the idea of what is called confetti money. But confetti money is a new currency invented to deal with workers' wages. We never hear the increases awarded to judges, field marshals or senior civil servants being described as confetti money. There seem to be two currencies in this country, the currency in which better-paid people are paid where the gain is held to be real and currency given to the working class which, they are told, is actually worthless. This is an aspect which destroys a great deal of credibility in presenting wage restraint as the key question. People are willing to see an element of wage planning as part of a planned economy but what is not acceptable is that wages should be planned but the salaries of professional people, people who live on dividends and those who are living on incomes which cannot be easily measured should be exempted and that prices should be exempted and that foreign trade or capital movements trade should be exempted from parallel developments in planning. This helps to undermine the credibility of any public statements made about the key importance of wage restraint in the recovery of the economy.

There will have to be joint planning of the economy. This was the basis of the 1974 manifesto. But the legislation for planning agreements and industrial democracy was not carried through. Sanctions, which could easily have been applied to bring about planning agreements, were confined to the function of controlling wages.

The Trade Union Role in Planning

The trade union movement would be prepared to play a bigger part in planning the economy seriously provided that its members are satisfied that something is going to be done. They are not prepared to do the necessary work, which is enormous, if at the end, like the Lucas Aerospace workers, they are going to be told that what they are seeking to do is to interfere with management prerogatives. We cannot approach the question of industrial democracy if people are told that, regardless of what they may discover about the firm in which they work, they are still going to be held to a general percentage. Then people go back to the old ways and say, 'Right, we will simply get as much as we can out of the firm in which we work, squeezing the orange until the pips squeak and we will do the same again next year'. With strong trade unions in an inter-dependent and vulnerable technical society this introduces pressure so great that it gives rise to a counter demand to restrain trade union power — which is what we saw in the early part of 1979, and earlier in 1974 during the miners' strike, or earlier still in 1968 with *In Place of Strife*.[3] The break-out from this involves going back to free collective bargaining, broadening the area of free collective bargaining to cover a wider range of issues that affect real living standards and the future of our manufacturing industry.

To some extent the trade union movement itself has to make the adjustment. Industrial democracy imposes a far greater strain on the trade union movement and its traditional structures than it does on management. In a curious way management has always argued that it would rather deal with its own employees than deal with national officials and if their own employees get together and create a joint shop stewards' committee and then come to the management, management may find that easier to deal with because they are then negotiating with people whose incomes come out of the same pool as themselves. When this is set against the national, regional, district and branch organisation of national trade unions, there can be serious difficulties. To this extent the trade union movement itself will have to adjust its own practices to find a way in which national, regional and branch officials can work more closely with joint shop stewards. The joint shop stewards movement contains the capacity to move the whole question of wage bargaining and company bargaining and even differentials on to a completely different level.

Combine committees[4] also present real difficulty for national trade unions. Active combines and shop stewards in some ways prefer operating in the context of the firm rather than going to the local district committee where their business will only be one of a number of items on the agenda. They may also find that they appear to have more in common with representatives of other unions in the same plant than either of them will have with the full-time officials in their own union. Combines which bring together all the joint shop stewards in one plant with similar workers in another plant, or those which spread across a whole industry, are a new form of trade unionism which appears to cut across the national and regional structure. This is something to which the trade union movement will have to give a lot of thought and it is not at all surprising that Lucas Aerospace came up against not only the hostility of those who believe in the management prerogative, but also imposed a very substantial strain upon the existing type of national trade union representation.

Planning agreements, by working towards joint representation committees (which would really be combines), would be giving statutory form to this new type of unionism. Increasingly the trade unions at shop floor level would see their regional officials as people with regional responsibilities and would see the TUC General Council as the parliament of labour engaged primarily in negotiating with government and employers about the general direction of economic, social, industrial policy and even international or Common Market policy. This process is going to take a long time to work out and one could find many examples of conflicts between the existing structure and these new workers' initiatives. Without compulsory planning agreements there will be no solution to the wage problem.

Workers' Co-ops

Workers' co-operatives could also play an important part in extending the control of people over all the circumstances of their working lives. This depends very largely on the degree of initiative from the workers themselves. You cannot build co-operatives from the top. What we have to do is make the co-operative option no more difficult than the other options available. Once you offer people a real option then they can choose to take it at the time when the defects in the old structure become apparent. A real co-operative option open to workers at the crucial moment during a pay claim, or under threat of redundancy or collapse or a merger, would change their prospects. That is the moment that people should be able to move over a bridge from the old type of industrial ownership and control to a new type of co-operative.

People will not turn their minds seriously to institutional change when everything is going all right. You wouldn't expect people in a successful company with a growing labour force, and rising living standards, to want to turn their factory upside down and run it differently. The trade union movement has operated for a long time on—to use management jargon—'management by exception'. Most top management don't interfere in the way the company is run by subordinates unless something goes wrong. The trade union movement has operated on a similar basis. They do not interfere with management unless something goes wrong. Then when something does go wrong, the question is what can they do about it. In wage negotiations under collective bargaining, labour has real power against capital because workers can withdraw their labour. When the firm goes bust they can't withdraw their labour because their labour has been taken from them anyway. Occupations, sit-ins, the planning of a co-operative—as happened at Upper Clyde Shipbuilders, at Meriden and Kirkby—were important because they revealed a readiness to extend the vision of labour beyond pay. Men at Meriden or the *Scottish Daily News* or Kirkby were transformed not by anything that was done by government, but by their readiness to take responsibility. There was the most *bitter* official hostility to what they were trying to do. I have never in the whole of my political life known the establishment devote so much time and effort to trying to frustrate any industrial initiative as they did with the co-operatives. At first I couldn't understand it. The reasons given to me were so unconvincing. They said this could 'damage the interests of co-operation'. 'Wouldn't it be better to get co-operatives going where they could be successful?' Those who said this didn't believe in co-operation anywhere, successful or unsuccessful. Then they said that this would be unfair to the people concerned as they were bound to fail. But the real reason was that if you open up an escape from the ordinary mechanism of market discipline which gives to the owners the ultimate power to sack, you have undermined the whole basis of capitalist discipline. Looking back on it I have no doubt whatsoever that those three co-operatives played a tremendous part in boosting the self-confidence of workers by showing them the possibility of another route. Without such practical examples, nothing can ever be done. You can pay academics to write about industrial democracy but it is better to use the money, not on funding professors, but on funding people who are prepared to do it. It was well worth while.

The producer co-op has a great deal to offer, particularly in small businesses and in what management would call 'small profit centres' in a big enterprise, such as a plant producing motor-car components for a big firm which might be made into a co-operative in its own right. The Co-operative Development Agency should be developed in the way in which it was first conceived,[5] that is to say, with a range of functions at least as great as that available to the old Industrial Reorganisation Corporation or to the National Enterprise Board, and with the appropriate funds.

Then, for example, the workers at Lucas Aerospace would have two possible options open to them. They could negotiate a compulsory planning agreement which would be linked to the government's support for that firm. This would transform the relationship between labour and management at Lucas. It would make the payment of government aid a part of a new structure under which the unions would be able to put their views forward on a whole range of issues concerned with the long-term future of the company; how much it would invest, the products it should make, and so on. Alternatively, we could support the initiative taken by the workers from Lucas Aerospace through a co-operative supported by government funds.

There are, however, dangers in a naive or emotional commitment to co-operation without analysing some of the problems. A new school of thought now developing within the Conservative Party and among industrialists looks at co-operatives in a way that creates new dangers for the trade unions. Some Conservatives would like workers to confront directly the disciplines of the market economy through co-operatives. In this way they hope to create a new framework in industry in which capital can withdraw to a banking function, only funding co-operatives that are successful in fighting market forces. This is also what lies behind 'market socialism'. Industrialists who are ready to fund co-operatives see this as a way to withdraw from their role as managers of labour in the front line, letting the workers fight market forces alone, only sending reinforcements in the form of capital investment to those who are prepared to accept the hazards themselves. This is a danger which the Labour Movement would be well advised to think about carefully.

A New Relationship between Labour and Capital

Co-operatives and planning agreements are only two options open to us in the battle to transform the relationship between capital and labour. In this area you cannot have a blue-print, you need a bag of tools. Provided the initiative is taken by the workers themselves then the capacity of the government to respond is infinite. When private industry comes to government, the government will underwrite risks, will pay redundancy money, will fund investment, will provide special environmental assistance or whatever. Modern British capitalism nestles in the all-embracing arms of a generous government, financed by the tax-payer. Labour by contrast is still living in the chill wind of competition. There is no reason on earth why that should be the case. It would be quite possible to extend to labour at least the same generosity that capital receives. Labour has the capacity to succeed providing capital is available, but capital can't do without the goodwill of labour. Labour in Britain is not revolutionary, but it 'works to rule' if it becomes convinced that management is not interested in the products it produces, but simple in the maximisation of profits short-term. That is no basis either for productivity or for the long-term future of a great manufacturing nation.

Our present economic difficulties are producing a quite different response from the slump of the 1920s and 1930s. In those days unemployment actually led to a drift away from trade union membership. The present difficulties have led to a strengthening of the unions. Even middle-level management has gone through a complete transformation in its attitude to trade unionism. They are discovering that when the crash comes their interests lie with other workers. They realise that public investment and public ownership, if need be, and industrial democracy are in their interests. Industrial managers now realise that their writ no longer runs if it is simply based on a commission handed to them by their owners. It must depend on consent from the workers and that is why participative management has become fashionable. In terms of real democracy participative management is a bit of a fraud, but it is recognition of the need for consent. If you require consent from people who themselves are self-confident and are demanding more than consent, then you will find some fusing of the interests of the professional manager with the shop steward or trade union organiser. When a company collapses even well-paid managers, who thought that they were above the need for any protection, will suddenly realise that they too are unemployed and that it is harder for a £15,000-a-year manager to find a job than it is for a skilled welder. All of a sudden a common interest becomes apparent. This process is consolidating the role of the trade unions. Then when you get professional management, scientific and technical staff, skilled and unskilled workers all welding themselves together into a combine committee as at Lucas Aerospace all the qualities and skills necessary for an 'alternative strategy and management' become available and things begin to change.

In Britain we have over a long period of struggle actually bred a quality of collective leadership within the trade union movement which is quite capable of assuming a leading role within the framework of democracy in a way which simply wouldn't have been true at the time of the General Strike in 1926.

The more one considers the potential impact upon the whole nature of our economy of democracy carried as far as we have discussed it, the more one is driven to the conclusion that we would be moving from a situation where capital hires labour to a situation where labour hires capital. Labour requires capital. It might have to get it from the government as the mining industry does today or it might have to get it from the market. Once labour hires capital there is really a change in balance of power and hence not only in the balance of power in industry, but the balance of power in society. A great deal of the private sector power that exists is expressed through a whole range of other types of organisation, including, we might argue, the legal framework in which society works, that reflects itself through the role of the judges; through the ownership of the media; the education system which, in one respect, is producing people to meet the needs of society based upon a certain pattern of ownership. We are not talking about minor changes.

8

The Common Market

The kind of changes we have just been discussing will only be possible if we retain control of the management of our economy and the conduct of our affairs. This will not be possible as long as we remain in the Common Market on the present terms. One of the motives for the British establishment wanting us so strongly to go into Europe was that they believed that the British people armed with the ballot box were going to become unmanageable, and the only power structure strong enough to control us would be an international power structure. Deep pessimism about the future has always been a major factor in the establishment's support for the EEC. Pessimism is a major unexplored force in Britain today. There is the pessimism of the ultra-left, but there is also a pessimism of the right which believes that Britain is finished and that the internationalisation of power must necessarily mean that we should subordinate our domestic democracy to the bureaucracy of international interdependence. There is also a conscious conception in the minds of some businessmen and financiers that if national democracy is allowed to mature and flower, as it could in Britain, it would become so powerful a force for social change that it could not be contained by the British financial and industrial establishment, which would need to call in aid from the powers of capital in Europe in order to hold it in restraint. That is what is meant by pessimistic federalism.

The Vichy spirit in the top echelons of the establishment is quite astonishing. If you listen to those who inhabit the golden triangle of the City of London, Fleet Street and Whitehall, there is a lot of defeatism. Compare that with the mood among shop stewards at Lucas Aerospace, at Meriden, at Kirkby,[1] at the shop stewards' committees up and down the country. They may be angry, worried, disappointed but they are not defeated. Compare them with the gloomy men who go to City luncheons and dinners in their boiled shirts for ever calling upon everybody else to face the harsh realities of technical change. It is a sort of 1984 in reverse.

There is no need to feel pessimistic about this country. It is only the upper echelons who are licked. For them the answer to Dean Acheson's suggestion that Britain had lost an Empire and hadn't discovered a new role is, 'Yes, we've discovered a role: we were an empire and now we will be a colony.' They are trying to transform the troublesome natives of Britain, whom they can't handle, into the subjects of a new imperialism. Imperialism of a more civilised, more urbane and bureaucratic kind, represented in their mind by the sort of federal Europe they would like to see created.

Three Criticisms of the EEC

Looking back on the argument on the Common Market, it is becoming clear that what the Labour Movement said about it in opposing our entry has turned out to be abundantly justified. All the fears have emerged in practice. Ours was not a nationalist but a democratic argument against membership. Where law-making power passes from a Parliament and a government you can replace, to a body of Commissioners whom you cannot replace, you have suffered a major loss of liberty. This was the first big move against the trend of universal adult suffrage and it is reinforced by the existence of the European Court.

The second warning that we gave has been proved correct too, namely that if a political constitution, the Treaty of Rome, has entrenched within it a legal definition of an aspiration to perfect a market economy it must necessarily represent a major defeat in the long march towards democratic socialism. And that has been proved time and again by the intervention of the Commission and the enforcement of its rulings by the European Court.

Over and above these criticisms involving bureaucracy and remoteness, there is a Cold War flavour about the Common Market. One of the motives behind its establishment was its role as a buffer state against Eastern Europe and as a replacement for American power in Western Europe lest it began to recede. There has been an anxiety that American power could not be relied upon for ever to sustain the economy and industry and society in Western Europe and that some domestic structure would be needed.

These three objections—that the Common Market was an instrument of bureaucracy, was wedded to capitalism, was divisive in Cold War terms and world peace terms—have all been justified. How it will develop from now on depends almost entirely on what we do about it. If we remain on present course, we might end up with a government driven to federalism by its own deep pessimism about the role of Britain. The form this would take we can already see because it has begun to happen already. First, through the more and more rigorous application of Common Market rules of internal free trade and free competition by the Commission, reinforced by the Court, possibly meeting resistance from the British government of the day, and gradually the replacement of our domestic law-making functions by Community law-making functions which could not then be repealed after a subsequent general election.

Second, the inevitable growth of bureaucracy and the extent to which our own civil service would attach themselves automatically to the stronger of two forces. If British officials had to choose between the waning power of British ministers and the British Parliament and the growing strength of the European bureaucracy, they would choose the latter. There has been a massive shift of power to ministers and officials and away from Parliament. Every minister who has a big volume of European business is represented on a whole host of committees in Europe by officials. It is one thing for a minister to get control of his government department in a domestic context (that is quite difficult) but to mastermind negotiations on a daily basis in Brussels on the end of a telex or telephone line is like trying to play chess ten feet away from the board and moving each piece with string. It can't easily be done. This move towards official control is a shift from Parliament to officials. If a minister wants to get a piece of legislation through the British Parliament officials have to prepare it, it has to go to other ministers, it has to get in the Queen's Speech, it has to go through first reading, second reading, committee stage, report stage, a third reading in both Houses; but if a minister can be sent to Brussels to do it secretly, that is much quicker. Civil servants and ministers will in future tend to go for the line of least resistance. The weight of legislation that comes to us from Brussels against the volume that comes through Parliament is going to tilt heavily towards Brussels.

Third, depending on how the world develops, there would be a growing tendency to allow the Common Market to develop in a military or quasi-military direction. This would begin with small and innocent advances such as international co-operation to deal with terrorism and bringing the security forces together. Of course NATO and the Common Market are not entirely co-terminous in their nature but the old proposals for a European Defence Community in 1955, indeed even Harold Wilson's ill-starred proposals of 1963 for a mixed-manned fleet, could reappear. They could create circumstances in which the sinews of Common Market sovereignty begin to assert themselves in the military field and we could find that the Commission had assumed the European responsibilities of NATO and was beginning to co-ordinate its military work. Once that happened, and it could easily happen over a period of a generation or two, then there would be a military force also capable of enforcing decisions of the European Court in support of the Treaty of Rome, if ever national opposition to the Court were to reach the point where it became insupportable. This is looking a long way ahead, but it would be foolish to leave out of account one possible direction of the European idea — not the one we shall necessarily follow — in the minds of those who so strongly advocated our membership and who were most sincerely and deeply motivated by the idea of European Federation in the immediate post-war period.[2]

As we have already seen, the effect of the EEC on our economy has been to weaken it. As an industrial power not capable of feeding ourselves the historic formula for British economic strength has been that in return for manufactured goods sold to the developing world we got cheap food. The effect of the Common Agricultural Policy in restricting the entry of less expensive food has handicapped us greatly. The opening up of a free market, free trade policy towards our most formidable competitors has meant, as we warned during the Referendum, that our ageing and ill-equipped industries have been increasingly pounded by the full weight of some of the most powerful industrial competition there is from inside the Community.

If the Common Market trading rules, enforced by the Commission and the Court, were to stop us channelling investment back into our industries from our own savings on the grounds that this prevented the development of free trade in the EEC, then we would find ourselves almost imprisoned in a pattern of decline from which there would be no recovery. Then British workers might have to seek employment on the Continent as guest-workers in some of the more successful European industries. These industries may in any case have been re-equipped by British money from the profits of British industry which find their way under the free movement of capital to the more successful economies, where the unions are weaker.

This is an attempt to analyse what was being said by the Labour Movement at the time of the referendum in the summer of 1975. In the light of our experience since, this would appear to be what is happening.

The campaign for the referendum began around 1968 and I was of the view that we should not enter Europe without the explicit assent of the people. Even Edward Heath said that we should not enter without the full-hearted consent of the Parliament and people—a pledge he broke. We had the referendum, but it came after we had entered, and therefore was really a vote on whether we wanted to leave. The referendum was an expression of the popular will at the time and had to be accepted in the way that you accept a general election result. But it is no part of any democratic argument that you must accept any defeat as final. It was a recognition that the British people, expressing themselves through the ballot box, did not wish to leave in the summer of 1975. But at least the principle of the legal sovereignty of the British Parliament has been entrenched and repeated even by pro-Market ministers and lawyers since then. Nobody has yet said — though it could happen later — that it would not be constitutional for the British Parliament to seek withdrawal. British ministers could use the prerogative of the Crown — for it was by that prerogative that we joined — to terminate our adherence to the Treaty.

What the Labour Party has done since the referendum[3] has been to develop an alternative perspective for Europe based upon the demand for the restoration of powers to the House of Commons to break the stranglehold of the Treaty and its application by the Commission. The party has also called for a fundamental review of the Treaty of Rome and the Common Agricultural Policy, and for British ministers to be made accountable to the House of Commons. We have also said that if, after a reasonable period, these changes have not been secured the Labour Party would feel free to consider whether it was in the interests of the British people to remain members of the Common Market. Were we to raise that question again, it would be expressed either in the form of an election campaign based upon withdrawal or some demand for fresh public consent for withdrawal. We are not committed to withdrawing now, nor are we committed to withdrawal in principle, but we have made it absolutely clear that, like any other policy, the policy of membership of the Common Market is open for review and reconsideration in the event of it being necessary that we should do so. That option will become of course progressively more difficult as the process of integration goes on, but it remains the basic democratic right of the British people.

If we remain inside the Community as it is now there is little hope of our achieving the social aspirations we have discussed elsewhere. This could not be done on the basis of the present Treaty, the present Commission, the present Court and the present structure. Britain has never had a written constitution before. The French, Germans and Italians have had written constitutions for many years and they often seem to work on the basis that you regard constitutions as interesting documents and then you do as you like. We are, by contrast, exceptionally law-abiding in Britain.

There is another aspect. Britain has the most powerful domestic democracy and strongest Labour Movement of any in Europe. For the French, German and Italian Socialists the Common Market represented an aspiration towards solidarity and peace after years of Nazi occupation and fascist regimes. For them, the Treaty, with all its defects, is a step forward; for us it was a step back. Britain is, to that extent, a century ahead of them in democratic experience. The arguments that the British Labour Movement will be putting forward in Europe are arguments that are going to carry great weight. Our analysis opens up the true interests of working people in Britain vis-à-vis the Community, and will be seen, in time, to be relevant for French, German and Italian workers too. The possibility that there are allies for what the British Labour Movement is saying should never be underestimated. Over a period a wider, looser socialist co-operation could be achieved within a reformed Community, or a Community which had simply decided to set aside the reactionary tendencies that inspired the founders of the Treaty of Rome.

9

Democracy

The story of British democracy is the conversion of privileges into rights. The way in which we seem to have proceeded over the centuries has been by periodic challenges, of varying intensity but long-term success, by the governed against the government. From the time of Runnymede when the barons won feudal rights from the King to the period of the revolution of 1649 when the gentry won rights from the feudal authorities, to the 1832 Reform Act when the new capitalist class won greater power for the middle class and the entrepreneur, to the battle for the franchise and votes for women, the story is the same: there has always been an enlargement of the area of actual decision-making.

The establishment at any one time is the body of key people whose assent is required to govern. The trade union leadership entered the establishment with the post-war Labour Government, having been a powerful but external force in pre-war years. The war made it necessary to include them when Ernest Bevin was Minister of Labour. Within the broad arena of consent that formal political democracy requires are to be found the key group of policy-makers. The next stage in the development of democracy must lie first of all in entrenching the rights already achieved. We have got to fight many of those old battles all over again. For example, the restoration of the use of the royal prerogative for Common Market purposes represents a massive reversal from parliamentary to executive control. The development of prime ministerial patronage also represents a reversal of a trend which was first set when Parliament insisted on appointing the Crown's advisers. Then the Cabinet ceased to be a royal coterie and was drawn from the leaders of the representatives in the House of Commons whose advice it was obligatory for the monarch to accept. Now the powers of monarchy, except in its formal sense, have passed to the Prime Minister and the massive scale of prime ministerial patronage now represents a new centre of executive power which must be controlled again by Parliament.

The argument about secrecy in government which was first fought when Edmund Burke in his earlier days campaigned for the publication of *Hansard* has been lost to the Official Secrets Act. The control of a standing army, which was finally settled in 1689 by the decision that the House of Commons would only vote money to the armed forces on an annual basis, has been lost with the development of the security services whose responsibility to Parliament is non-existent.

There is another aspect of the democratic struggle: the role of the media. In the old days the powers of the medieval Church to put a priest in every pulpit of every parish on every Sunday to preach to the faithful the view of an established Church reinforced the power of the monarch. This was challenged by the dissenters who said, 'We want the right to elect our own lecturers.' This is a battle which has to be fought and won again.

The first stage in the battle for democracy must be to re-examine critically what has happened, including the loss of powers to the Common Market and say, 'We want those powers back again.' Beyond that, to win back the powers that have passed to the new monarch, the new priesthood, the new Church and the military will involve formidable arguments. These must be resolved not only in a parliamentary context, but inside the Labour Movement where new feudal baronies can be created, and inside the parliamentary Labour Party and the party itself. That is the first stage.

The next stage must be to develop and advance still further from that point. The battle to be fought in the future will be about open government; a proper democratic supervision of the bureaucracy, the military and the security services. We need free media to allow people to have access to each other instead of having to rely upon the present control mechanisms.

The public ownership of knowledge is also one way of describing the development of comprehensive life-long education to allow us all to have access to it. We must re-establish the very simple principle that the moral authority for power must rest on the consent of the governed as institutionally safeguarded by elective bodies. The powers of selection and reselection need to be entrenched in the Constitution both of the country and of the Labour Movement. This will all be necessary if we are to achieve the gradual assertion of human values against the forces of capital and bureaucracy. All these things must be brought about in the 1980s. The whole drift of the argument on the Left is towards democracy and not, as is asserted by the Right, towards dictatorship. 1984 arrived earlier than expected and characterises the Right, not the Left.

Open Government

The specific changes necessary to democratise our society must include, first, open government. There is no doubt whatever that if the Prime Minister was obliged to disclose to the House of Commons and through them to the public the proceedings of the government and the papers that are prepared by officials, this would lead to a reinforcement of democratic power, both over ministers and civil servants and over the European Commission.

There should be a statutory right of access to public documents so that people know what's happening. Everyone accepts the need to maintain secrecy on matters of high military security or commercial confidentiality or the personal records of individuals which, though protected from the public gaze, should be disclosed to them so they can check inaccuracies, malice or prejudice in them.

Second, parliamentary select committees should be able to interrogate ministers and officials. Third, Parliament and its committees should be televised so that the power of the press to present Parliament through the biased eyes of their own proprietors would be substantially broken. Fourth, the House of Lords should be abolished as an obsolete and unnecessary part of our constitution. Then within the Labour Party there should be parallel developments: democratic accountability to ensure that a Prime Minister is more closely accountable to the party; where the Cabinet are elected by the parliamentary party; the closer accountability of the people at the top in the trade union movement and the Labour Party to their rank and file in the constituencies or the shop stewards' movement; recognition of the rights of the shop steward organisation in the Labour Movement and of the importance of constituency party active members in the development of policy through conference and its implementation. All these changes are now firmly on the agenda and they will really transform British politics and deepen and strengthen British democracy. If we are prepared to campaign from below our democracy will be much more strongly rooted in the desires and needs of our people.

Take, for instance, the proposal for the annual election of the Cabinet.[1] Here the first move is to replace the present appointment of the Cabinet by the election, preferably by open voting, of a parliamentary committee when Labour is in government in the same way as we elect it when we are in opposition. The effect of that would not necessarily be a change in the composition of the Cabinet, though there might be some changes, but it would be the difference in the relationship between the Cabinet and the parliamentary party that would matter. Whereas now all Cabinet ministers look up to their patron, the Prime Minister, and are over-influenced by his or her approval or disapproval, for he or she alone has the power to promote or displace them, they would be looking to their constituents (the MPs) upon whose consent they depend for the passage of their legislation. It would mean that instead of a Cabinet of twenty-three placemen and two elected leaders, there would be an elected body with a collectivity arising from their common constituency. It would mean that reshuffles would be carried through by the parliamentary party in the light of the record of ministers and not by the Prime Minister according to personal preference. It would mean the general disclosure of papers within the Cabinet because instead of one person, albeit the leader, having the sole right of access to all Cabinet papers they would be the property of the whole Cabinet. It would mean that backbench members faced with government legislation that they did not like would not be tortured by the dilemma of voting against their conscience and party policy on the one hand or voting to bring down the government on the other. They would express their views in the annual election of the Cabinet and might choose to replace the minister concerned when the opportunity next presented itself. All ministers would be well aware of this when they presented their legislation. It would transform the democracy of the Labour Party. And Labour MPs, who are now subject to the extra discipline of reselection and are excluded by our party constitution from formulating policy (which is a function of the National Executive), would at least have the authority to keep a Labour government accountable to them for what they say they would do and are required to do. This would do much to revitalise and strengthen the morale, the role and the importance of the parliamentary Labour Party. And if, as should happen, the voting for the Cabinet was published—as are Commons division lists—then there would be full accountability.

The Unions

Democracy in the unions is important too, but it must be left to internal pressure within the trade union movement. The idea of an external parliamentary force democratising trade unions when no such force has been used to democratise the power of business or finance would be an outrage. The difference between forcing an external 'democratisation' on the unions and having it carried through by internal forces from below would be tremendous. External forces would be designed to entrench the leadership against the rank and file, internal forces to build up the position of the rank and file vis-à-vis the leadership. These things will come but they must be achieved without damaging the legitimacy of trade union leaders who are, after all, already much more democratically elected than the chairman of the BBC, the chairman of the Stock Exchange or the Governor of the Bank of the England with whom they deal. They must be achieved in a way that provides no

ammunition for an anti-trade union campaign, which some
would like to promote because the trade unions are a precious
source of strength for working people.

The Armed Forces

We must also consider the role the armed forces should play in
a democracy. They have an influence that extends far beyond
the air fields, naval bases and barracks in which they are
situated. They are very big spenders, commanding a mass of
industrial, scientific and academic expertise which works for
them and is equally committed to their continued budgetary
growth. They operate in secrecy on the grounds that secrecy is
inseparable from security. The armed forces are disciplined
hierarchies which, alone among modern organisations,
explicitly and categorically deny to their employees rights of
citizenship which any industrial, clerical or administrative
workers would regard as his natural right. Servicemen have the
vote, but no right to speak, to organise any trade unions, to
criticise or discuss any decisions by their officers, or to
enter into the normal processes of public argument about their
own role or the direction of society. The military has established a position within every modern society that must
necessarily impinge upon the role of elected governments,
even where the generals accept that they are under political
control. Yet we cannot know, because these things are secret,
what are the influences brought to bear by the military upon
political leaders. The control of the military by democratically
elected members of Parliament and responsible government is
an integral part of our own parliamentary tradition. It goes
back to the settlement of 1689 when William III came to the
throne at the invitation of Parliament after James II had fled.
From that time onwards the provision of money for the armed
forces was made by the Annual Parliamentary Grant. The
Army Annual Act was the means by which Parliament controlled the disciplinary powers of the armed forces to be sure
that the military never seized power.

This ultimate safeguard is not fully understood by everyone
in this country, but it is important. It is as important now as it

was three hundred years ago that the military should be under parliamentary control and that we should know that the reason for it is internal and not external. What has happened since the Glorious Revolution of 1688 is that technology has shifted the balance of power more sharply towards the military in every country, and we must not allow it to displace democratic accountability. The parallel between the old standing army and the modern security services is that in the old days armies were rarely used for foreign wars, but were primarily instruments of domestic repression. When Parliament demanded control of the army it was actually saying it wanted control of the security services. The internal role of the security services and the armed forces must be restricted by democratic control in any country which wishes to avoid the remote possibility of a military takeover at any time when that nation is facing difficulties. To say this merely emphasises a hallowed and existing part of our constitution: it is not adumbrating any new development or policy for democratic government.

The Media

Then there is the question of democratising the media. In *The People and the Media*[2] we talked about a National Printing Corporation and the possibility that the government might own and make available facilities for printing so that different views could be expressed through Labour and other papers. The trade union movement could itself take the role of a proprietor and promote a newspaper by carrying losses as some proprietors have done. The trade union movement should seriously consider this. The danger from the media is so great now that a Labour paper or papers even at relatively high cost has now become a priority. One of the interesting things about our industrial system at the moment is that whereas the trade union movement has always been responsive in character it is now beginning to take the initiative and actually propose solutions to industrial problems and it has got the expertise and capacity to push those solutions. It should begin with the trade union movement launching a national newspaper. It does not follow at all that even if deprived of advertising for a time, or

176

perhaps for ever, there would not be a very big market for such a body of opinion.

In *The People and the Media* there were plans for an Advertising Revenue Board which would tax newspaper advertising money and re-allocate the proceeds to help launch papers of various opinions. Perhaps access to a National Printing Corporation should be free, as it is to our public libraries and museums and for the same reason. Perhaps money made available to the National Printing Corporation should be on the same scale as is available to the Arts Council, or the Social Science Research Council, or the University Grants Committee. All this could be thought about. What has first to be determined is whether this is the right approach and, if so, the necessary will and effort has to be put behind it.

The BBC is far too big. It was set up to produce one national radio programme and only later did it move into television and overseas broadcasting. There is a case for restructuring the BBC to permit greater diversity of view within it. The future structure of the BBC was referred to in the 1978 White Paper[3] published by the Home Office and it includes some potentially progressive suggestions, including the idea of separate boards for the BBC, leaving the power of the governors to supervise the managing directors and these boards who should be appointed separately. That is certainly a move in the right direction.

A proper examination of broadcasting would have to take account of a number of other factors. One is the method of financing of the BBC. The licence is little more than a regressive poll tax. The Labour Party is committed to a phasing out of the licence fee. We should also look at the financing of the programme contractors within commercial television. They are in fact not programme contractors at all, in that they do not make and sell programmes. National air time for advertising is contracted to them and they make programmes out of that money.

The technology of broadcasting is also changing very rapidly now. The scope for decentralised broadcasting and television with much cheaper equipment is opening up and how all that is used is very important. It could be shaped in one way so it all goes commercial like the lowest end of Fleet Street, or it could be shaped in such a way as to carry the public service tradition into the new television channels which will emerge. New technology and the way it is handled has other important implications for democracy. One of the frightening things about high technology is that, because it requires a high degree of scientific education in those who work in it, a new priesthood develops. The scientific community is inclined to say 'Oh, you don't know anything about this. It's all very complicated. You've got to do it this way.' Having been a minister in high technology industries over a long period I am continually struck by the reluctance, in some cases blank refusal, of people to confide to a minister, who they do not think can be trusted to understand what it is all about, information that is absolutely necessary for the political supervision of what is done. If we fail to insist on explanations and adopt centralised or technocratic solutions, we will come unstuck sooner or later. We must never accept that democracy can be limited by the educational qualifications of the rank and file. Once you take that view you have abandoned the whole battle for democracy at the very moment when its beneficient influence is most necessary.

A New Role for Political Leaders

It naturally follows from this argument that the role of political leadership is likely to change in a number of significant ways in the years ahead, drawing their power less from the executive authority they have acquired by election and more from influence, helping people to see what they can achieve for themselves. Dissenters must be protected. They must be protected from witch-hunters, from the heretic burners, from the Thought Police, from the Ecclesiastical Courts, from the KGB, from the CIA, from MI5 and Special Branch who in this country as in any country in the world are always looking for difficult men who may be saying something that in some way undermines the authority of society. This is not a charter for anarchism, nor a dream of creating a wholly self-regulating economic and political system. Leadership there must be, but not all from the top. Leadership is inseparable from responsibility and responsibility is inseparable from power, and if power is now being disseminated more widely, leadership will have to be more widely shared too.

More than five hundred years before the birth of Christ, Lao-Tzu, the Chinese philosopher, had this to say about leadership:

> As for the best leaders, the people do not notice their existence. The next best the people honour and praise. The next the people fear, and the next the people hate. But when the best leader's work is done the people say, 'We did it ourselves.'

To create the conditions that will allow the people to do it themselves is the central task of leadership today.

Sources

1 *The Inheritance of the Labour Movement*

'The Levellers', a speech given at Burford Church in Oxfordshire, to a branch of the Workers' Educational Association, in May 1976.

'Marxism and the Labour Party', a speech given to Bristol University Labour Club in December 1976. Also published in the *Guardian*.

'Clause IV' — a commentary, taken from 'The Labour Party', by Tony Benn, unpublished.

2 *Labour's Industrial Programme*

The current work of the Department of Industry, TUC–Labour Party Liaison Committee, May 1974, for details of NEB and planning agreements.

'Subsidies for Private Industry', speech at Bristol May Day celebrations, May 5th 1974.

Hansard, February 2nd 1975, for details of funds available to the NEB.

Hansard, June 20th 1974, for details of comparative investment performance of UK and major competitors.

Speech at conference on 'The Future of the City of London', organised by the *Financial Times* and the *Investors Chronicle*, June 6th 1973.

Speech on industrial policy, Labour Party Conference, October 2nd 1973.

'The Labour Movement and The Public Sector — a Reassessment', Herbert Morrison Lecture, June 7th 1976.

'The Industrial Context', speech at the Institute for Workers' Control meeting, Blackpool, September 28th 1975, giving details of UCS and the co-operatives.

'Industrial Democracy', IWC pamphlet no. 45, Tony Benn's speech at the November 1974 Labour Party Conference IWC meeting.

'The Miners' Next Step', statement at the NUM Forum, Harrogate, December 7th 1977.

3   *Energy*

Speech on British oil policy delivered at Salomon Brothers, New York, April 5th 1977.

House of Commons speech on nuclear energy, *Hansard*, December 2nd 1977, cols 970–980.

Speech at Chatham House at the opening of a conference on oil and economic power, September 20th 1978.

House of Commons speech on the Windscale debate, *Hansard*, May 5th 1978, cols 172–178.

Interview with Tony Montague of *Whole Earth*, January 8th 1978.

Speech at the National Union of Mineworkers' annual conference in Torquay, July 5th 1978.

Speech to the Parliamentary Liaison Group for Alternative Energy Strategy, January 29th 1979.

Address to inaugural meeting of the Science, Technology and Society Association, February 3rd 1979.

4   *The EEC*

Statement of case against the EEC, *Encounter*, January 1963.

Speech given to the Deutsche Gesellschaft fur Auswärtige Politik, February 20th 1968.

Letter to constituents, November 1970, calling for referendum.

Speech to American correspondents in London, March 5th 1975, on the difference between the EEC and the United States of America.

Letter to constituents, December 29th 1974, setting out the benefits of parliamentary democracy which would be put at risk by membership of the EEC, published by the Anti-Common Market League, 1975.

Loss of control over the UK's industry and trade: speech in the City Hall, Glasgow, April 15th 1975.

Examples of EEC interference in British energy policy: speech at a Social Science Research Council meeting, London, July 18th 1978, and to the National Coal Board Advanced Management Course, July 24th 1978.

Unemployment: article in *The Times*, May 16th 1975; estimate of number of jobs lost given at a press conference of the National Referendum Campaign, May 18th 1975; further details from press statement issued May 26th 1975.

Assessment of four years' membership given at the Labour Common Market Safeguards Committee, Waldorf Hotel, London, June 2nd 1977.

Note: for a succinct summary of the case against the EEC see 'The Common Market', published in June 1978 by the Labour Common Market Safeguards Committee, 72 Albert Street, London NW1.

5 *Democracy*

Introduction to the 1929–31 Cabinet minutes, published by the Institute for Workers' Control, 1976.

The Right To Know, a lecture to the British Association for the Advancement of Science at Bath University, September 8th 1978.

Review of Harold Wilson's book *The Governance of Britain, Bristol Evening Post,* October 29th 1976.

Speech on Parliamentary Reform to a Press Gallery lunch at the House of Commons, February 14th 1977.

Statement announcing candidature for the leadership of the Labour Party, March 17th 1976; see also a further press release on March 18th.

The case for an inquiry into the security services was first made to a meeting of the Labour Party Home Policy Sub-Committee, October 30th 1978.

Notes

All notes are by the Editor

1 *The Inheritance of the Labour Movement*

1 Pelican 1960, p. 157.
2 Mary Jessup, *History of Oxfordshire*, Phillimore 1975, p. 68.
3 Christopher Hill, *The World Turned Upside Down*, Penguin 1975, p. 17.
4 See pp. 28.
5 Cited in Hill, op. cit., pp. 132-3.
6 The Levellers were one of the several groups of radical pamphleteers who, in the wake of the English Civil War (1647-50), tried to promote a far-reaching social revolution. They drew up a political programme which anticipated by two centuries most other demands for radical change in Britain. They even made some headway in infiltrating Cromwell's army. This led to a mutiny in May 1649 which was quickly suppressed and a number of leading Levellers executed.

For detailed accounts see: H. N. Brailsford, *The Levellers and the English Revolution*, ed. Christopher Hill, Spokesman 1976; Hill, op. cit.
7 The full text is to be found in Professor D. M. Wolfe (ed.), *Leveller Manifestos of the Puritan Revolution*, Nelson 1944.
8 The name given to the army organised by Parliament on February 15th 1645.
9 This section is based on a speech made at Bristol University Labour Club in December 1976 following the controversy over the appointment of Andy Bevan, a Marxist, as the Labour Party National Youth Officer. The national press immediately seized upon the appointment to mount an hysterical campaign against Marxists in the Labour Party.
10 Gollancz, p. 26.
11 Harold Laski, *Marx and Today*, New Fabian Research Bureau, p. 1.
12 Ibid., p. 25.
13 Ibid., p. 28.

14 Donoughue, Bernard, and Jones, George William, *Herbert Morrison*, Weidenfeld and Nicolson 1973, p. 18.
15 Ibid., p. 19.
16 Michael Foot, *Aneurin Bevan 1945–1960*, Paladin 1975, p. 560.
17 *Tribune*, March 15th 1940.
18 *Briefe und Gespräche*, 'Letters and Discussions', Europäische Verlagsanstalt, extracts published in the *New Statesman*, September 17th 1976.
19 SCM Press 1965, p. 46.
20 Labour Party Constitution, available from Transport House.
21 Clause IV's continuing vitality was proved when, at the 1959/60 Party Conference, an attempt was made by Hugh Gaitskell and others to persuade the party to abandon it and to substitute a form of words that would have drained the party of its socialism, separated it from its history, and divided it in two. The attempt failed and Clause IV remains in the party's Constitution to this day.

2 *Labour's Industrial Programme*

1 Labour's Programme, 1973, p. 7.
2 The Labour Party's Manifesto 1974 (February), pp. 10–11.
3 The Labour Party's Manifesto, October 1974, p. 13.
4 From the 1973 Labour Party Conference report, pp. 166–7.
5 The Lonrho case arose from the revelation that the company's part-time chairman, the Conservative MP Duncan Sandys, was receiving his £38,000-a-year salary through a bank in the Cayman Islands.
6 Hoffman–La Roche were found to be charging the National Health Service £370 and £922 a kilo for drugs which were being sold in Italy for £9 and £20 respectively.
7 See Stuart Holland, *The Socialist Challenge*, Quartet 1975, pp. 49–50. Holland cites projections by the National Institute for Economic and Social Research (NIESR), Newbold and Jackson and S. J. Prais. Those quoted here are from Professor Prais.
8 'De-industrialisation in the UK, Background Statistics', NIESR Discussion Paper No. 23, Table 5.
9 *UN Monthly Bulletin of Statistics*: December 1962 (Special Table F); December 1967 (Special Table D); December 1968 (Special Table I).
10 'De-industrialisation in the UK', loc. cit., Table 2.
11 *Hansard*, January 20th 1978, cols 407–8; see also *Hansard*, February 2nd 1979, oral answers: assistance to the private

sector totalled approximately £5,000m from April 1st 1974 up to and including forecasts for 1978–9.

12 For a detailed list of the information a planning agreement should contain, see Holland, op. cit., pp. 228–9.

13 In practice little of this worked out as intended. The proposals which emerged were substantially different from those in the Labour Party manifesto. The difference has been summarised by Tom Forester in his article 'How Labour's industrial strategy got the chop' (*New Society*, July 6th 1978):

> Planning agreements were by now entirely voluntary. The government hadn't even taken reserve powers to ensure compliance after default and cash handouts to major companies were not tied to planning agreements. On the NEB front, the government had failed to take powers for the compulsory purchase of companies and the funds available to the NEB (£1,000m over an indefinite period) were inadequate since the original aim was to *double* manufacturing investment ... It was so short of funds that it could do no other than become simply a repository for bankrupt 'lame ducks' ... Benn had kept the right of the NEB to take over profitable manufacturing firms, but it didn't have the cash to do it.

As for Mr Benn himself, after a massive and highly personal press campaign against him (some of it co-ordinated from within the Cabinet itself), he was removed from the Department of Industry.

The consequences of all this have also been summarised by Tom Forester (*New Society*, ibid.):

> Investment has not picked up, in spite of Harold Wilson's restoration of 'business confidence' by sacking Benn, emasculating the NEB and back-pedalling on planning agreements. Moreover the collapse of British industry ... has accelerated: whole sectors like consumer electronics and consumer durables ... have been nearly wiped out.

One of the reasons for Labour's failure to implement the industrial programme on which the 1974–9 governments were elected was that not simply did party policy not have the support of the Labour leadership, but in some cases it was actively undermined by the leadership. In an interview with the *Guardian* journalist Terry Coleman, Harold Wilson gave a graphic illustration of the way in which he worked against the policies being put forward by the National Executive. Mr Coleman wrote (*Guardian*, October 15th 1976):

> Then we got round to the Labour Party National Executive and Sir Harold's letters to himself. He said a sub-committee of a sub-committee of the executive proposed to nationalise certain insurance companies. Now, I might think this was cynical, but he ... dictated a letter first to himself and then a reply from himself. He sent both to the insurance people saying they might like to send him his own letter and that his reply would then be published to show that the proposal was not government policy. A few months later he did the same with the merchant banks.

14 *National Income and Expenditure 1967–1977*, HMSO 1978, Table 1.11.

15 *Hansard*, June 17th 1914, col. 1140.

16 The Coal Industry Commission 1919, vol. I, Cmd 359, p. 324.

17 Minister of Transport 1931; Minister of Supply and Home Secretary in War Cabinet; Deputy Prime Minister 1945–51.

18 Salford have helped to rescue a pickle factory; Wandsworth, before losing control to the Tories in the 1978 borough elections, helped establish a local electronics co-operative. For a detailed account of what local authorities can do to encourage industry, see the Institute for Workers' Control bulletin no. 4, 1978, article by Michael Ward.

19 Upper Clyde Shipbuilders was allowed to go bankrupt in July 1971 after the Tories refused further government aid. The response of the UCS workers was to occupy the yard. The occupation lasted for seven months and ended with the Conservatives reversing their decision to end government aid. For a full account see Willie Thompson and Finlay Hart, *The UCS Work-In*, Lawrence and Wishart 1972.

20 Cmnd 2937, March 24th 1966.

21 For a detailed account see *The New Worker Cooperatives*, Spokesman 1976.

22 Meriden had been a motor cycle factory owned by BSA. After BSA collapsed in 1973 the plant was taken over by Norton Villiers Triumph, with the aid of loans and grants from the Conservative Government totalling nearly £5 million. Shortly afterwards the owner of NVT, Mr Dennis Poore, announced he was closing Meriden and declared its 1,750 workers redundant. The workers resisted and after a long struggle about one-third of them established their own co-operative with financial

backing from the Department of Industry. For a detailed account see *Sunday Times Magazine*, June 4th 1978.

23 Kirkby Manufacturing and Engineering, otherwise known as Fisher Bendix of Kirkby near Liverpool. After passing through a succession of private hands this company went bankrupt in 1974. After a two-week sit-in, Tony Benn, as Secretary for Industry, gave the workers £3.9 million in grants to set up their own co-operative. More than half the money had to go to the firm's owners for the lease of plant and machinery. The co-op was forced to close in April 1979.

24 Shotton and Shelton were two steel plants faced with closure.

25 Chairman of the British Steel Corporation.

26 For details see the Bristol Aircraft Workers, 'A New Approach to Public Ownership', Institute for Workers' Control, pamphlet no. 43.

3 *Energy*

1 Not to mention the Tories. In November 1977 Hugh Dykes, Conservative MP for East Harrow, revealed details of an attempt by some Conservatives to persuade the EEC Commission to take action against BNOC on the grounds that it was in breach of the Treaty of Rome. Had they succeeded in having BNOC crippled or dismantled the sole beneficiaries would have been the multinational oil companies whose obligations to safeguard British national interest would have been removed. Britain's North Sea oil revenues would have melted away. The Tories were apparently prepared to use their contacts with the EEC to help the oil companies at the expense of Britain. Nothing further seems to have come of this episode, so far.

2 Responsibility for the planning aspects of this decision was eventually transferred to the Environment Secretary, Peter Shore, although Tony Benn was closely involved in the debates that led up to it and supported this change.

3 Coal Board plans to mine the large quantities of coal under the beautiful Vale of Belvoir in Leicestershire are to be the subject of a public inquiry. Ekofisk was an oil well in the North Sea which in April 1977 got out of control and spurted thousands of gallons of oil into the sea.

4 The Windscale Inquiry, report published by HMSO, January 26th 1978.

5 The contract for uranium was signed by the UK Atomic Energy Authority.

6 Jock Dunn, Area Secretary of the Kent Mineworkers, wrote an

attack on the government's fuel policy. His view was the basis of the response by the National Union of Mineworkers to the policy of running down the mining industry. He was writing in December 1967 — six years before the OPEC countries drastically increased the price of their oil:

> We believe that the government policy of increasing dependence on oil is fraught with danger ... We think the assumptions relating to oil prices in the future are based on completely baseless and illogical reasoning, and certainly not related to the reality of the new developing situation in the Middle East ...
> Our privileged position in the Middle East has largely been obtained and retained by power, and unlike the government we think the situation is changing and will continue to change ... We do not think it necessary to be political theoreticians to estimate that the people of the Middle East, who, like ourselves, are anxious to assure and improve their standards of living, will in fact demand just that. This eventually can change the whole relationship of oil prices with other fuels, and long-term represents a critical economic factor in the costing of the nation's fuel.

7   Britain now accounts for about one-third of all EEC investment in coal. We also produce the cheapest coal in Europe. According to figures supplied by the EEC Commission the cost of coal per tonne in 1977 in Germany was £37; Belgium £50; France £37 and in Britain £22. The same document provided figures for the subsidies which each country gives to its coal industry. See Table 5.

Table 5

Country	Aid to current production		Aid not related to current production*
	Total £m	Aid/tonne £	Total £m
Belgium	167	23·86	403
France	293	14·65	768
Germany	504	5·73	1,733
UK	26	0·21	49

* The figures in this column for the other countries contain monies which in the UK may be covered by the Social Security system.

8 For details of planning agreements see pp. 55–7.

9 3rd and 4th Reports published July 25th and 28th 1977, House of Commons 534/1 and 564/1.

10 The idea for a barrage across the River Severn has been discussed for about forty years and at the time of writing is being considered by a committee under the government's chief scientist, Sir Herman Bondi. Although such a barrage would be extremely expensive it could generate enough electricity to take the place of about four nuclear power stations.

4 The EEC

1 *Encounter*, January 1963.

2 Extract from a speech given to the Deutsche Gesellschaft für Auswärtige Politik in Bonn, February 20th 1968.

3 *Historical Review of Pennsylvania*, 1759.

4 EEC Energy Commissioner.

5 Taken from 'The Common Market', a pamphlet published by the Labour Common Market Safeguards Committee, June 1978. The figures do not include Ireland and Denmark.

6 Overseas Trade Statistics.

7 The pro-Common Market campaign, Britain in Europe, received individual contributions totalling £996,000, mainly from industry and the City. Of this they spent £587,000 on advertising, £265,000 on printing and £136,000 on salaries and expenses for people they employed for the campaign. By contrast, the anti-Market referendum campaign received individual donations of just £8,600. Both sides also received £125,000 each from the government. For detailed accounts see the *Financial Times*, October 8th 1975.

8 Table 6 shows the size of the EEC food mountains — created by buying up 'surplus' food in order to keep the price artificially high — by 1978.

Table 6

Commodity	tonnes
Skimmed milk powder	1,046,200
Butter	159,700
Beef	353,600
Cereals	1,094,600

Source: Written answer, *Hansard*, December 1st 1977, cols 47–48. The estimated cost of the subsidies involved was about £5,900 million.

9 See page 104.
10 UK Balance of Payments 1966–77, Central Statistical Office, p. 54.
11 Table 7 shows the details.

Table 7

Year	Gross contribution £ m	Receipts £ m	Net contribution £ m
1978	1,120	460	660
1979	1,235	470	765
1980	1,320	490	830
1981	1,280	490	790
1982	1,295	495	800

All figures at 1977 Survey Prices.
Source: Written answer, *Hansard*, January 12th 1978, col. 793.

12 BBC Radio 4, November 27th 1976.

5 *Democracy*

1 Published by the Institute for Workers' Control.
2 Michael Joseph 1976, p. 167–8.
3 Extract from a lecture given by Vice-President (then Senator) Mondale, delivered at the Kansas Law School, November 1976.
4 As Prime Minister, Mr Callaghan seemed to be under the impression that he had complete personal discretion as regards collective Cabinet responsibility. On June 16th 1977, he was asked by the Leader of the Opposition, Mrs Thatcher, to comment on reports that collective responsibility would be lifted for the EEC direct election campaign (as it had been for the referendum campaign on Common Market entry in 1975). Mr Callaghan replied as follows: ' ... I certainly think that the doctrine should apply, except in cases where I announce that it does not.' This statement removed the idea that collective Cabinet responsibility is a fact of the constitution of the United Kingdom.
5 Figures supplied by the House of Commons Library.
6 November 30th 1976.
7 On the contrary, for all the rhetoric about the need for greater openness most Prime Ministers seem as determined as ever to maintain secrecy. On November 10th 1978, the *New Statesman* published a minute from the Prime Minister to members of his

Cabinet in which he set out his reasons for not allowing ministers even to disclose the existence, never mind the business, of Cabinet committees. Among the reasons given was the possibility that 'Select Committees might try to summon the Chairmen of Cabinet Committees to give evidence ... and there would be questions about when the Committees were meeting, the work they were doing, whether particular ministers are on them ... ' Mr Callaghan concluded his revealing insight into the official attitude towards disclosure by saying that any departure from the existing convention of secrecy 'would be more likely to whet appetites rather than to satisfy them'.

8   Figures supplied by the House of Commons Library.

9   Figures supplied by the House of Commons Library.

10 Evidence that this concern may be justified was supplied by the journalist Chapman Pincher in his book *Inside Story*, (Sidgwick and Jackson, 1978). Mr Pincher writes that MI5 have files on more than two million people (p. 26); that our security services apparently believe 59 Labour MPs in the 1974–79 Parliament have 'current or recent connections with Communist, Trotskyist and other Marxist organisations' (p. 28); he also reports that 'certain officers inside MI5, assisted by others who had retired from the service, were actually trying to bring down the Labour government and in my opinion, they could at one point have succeeded ... ' (pp. 16–17).

11 In the Bill of Rights of 1689, Parliament decreed, among other things, that the raising or keeping by the monarch of a standing army in time of peace without the consent of Parliament is illegal.

7   Jobs

1   See p. 53.

2   For example, according to *Incomes Data Report* train-drivers, one of the most militant and best organised groups of trade unionists, achieved wage increases totalling 88 per cent on basic rates in the four years from April 1973 to April 1977. Despite this, the real net earnings of a train driver (after inflation) at 1973 prices went from £24.51 to £21.92 – a drop of nearly 10 per cent.

3   An unsuccessful attempt by the then Labour Government to reform the law relating to trade unions. Cmnd 3888, 1968/9.

4   Combine committees are formed by shop stewards representing

workers in different unions, but all working in the same plant or industry.

5 Many people hoped that the CDA, which was set up in September 1978, would be controlled by representatives elected from the co-op movement and would have resources to assist the setting up of worker co-ops. In fact its officers are all government appointed and the resources at its disposal are negligible.

8 *The Common Market*

1 Workers at Lucas Aerospace have produced a series of blueprints for converting their factories out of the production of armaments and into socially useful production. Kirkby and Meriden are worker co-ops set up in Liverpool and Birmingham. For further details, see p. 66.

2 The former Conservative minister, John Davis, made a speech in 1970 in which he spelled out clearly the military and political case for joining the Common Market. He said:

> What are we going to get out of it? Firstly, in a world where more and more the big battalions hold sway, we are going to move closer and closer to those who are not only our neighbours but who, for so many reasons, have interests compatible with our own. I know it is unfashionable to talk about the political objectives of the European community, but they seem to me by far the most important of all. Tensions on our continent's eastern, south-eastern and southern frontiers have not disappeared and, unhappily, are not likely to do so in the near future. The defence bulwark of the USA is to be gradually withdrawn. Western Europe, grudgingly and unenthusiastically no doubt, must unite to assure the safety of its own frontiers and, no less important, its strategic negotiating strength. The first thing we buy is, to my mind, the economic unity upon which must be built the political structure capable of assuring the independence of our continent and its right to develop its own particular mixture of democracy, liberalism and the respect of the individual.
>
> So number one on my list is the defence of the integrity of Western Europe towards which the enlargement of the community is the fourth faltering step after NATO, the Rome Treaty and the creation of EFTA.

3 Notably in the Manifesto for the European Elections which was agreed by the party National Executive in January 1979.

9 *Democracy*

1 As formally proposed by a large group of Labour MPs in early 1979.
2 Report of a Labour Party Study Group published by the Labour Party in 1974.
3 Cmnd 7294, published July 1978.

Index

MORE ABOUT PENGUINS, PELICANS
AND PUFFINS

For further information about books available from Penguins please write to Dept EP, Penguin Books Ltd, Harmondsworth, Middlesex UB7 0DA.

In the U.S.A.: For a complete list of books available from Penguins in the United States write to Dept DG, Penguin Books, 299 Murray Hill Parkway, East Rutherford, New Jersey 07073.

In Canada: For a complete list of books available from Penguins in Canada write to Penguin Books Canada Ltd, 2801 John Street, Markham, Ontario L3R 1B4.

In Australia: For a complete list of books available from Penguins in Australia write to the Marketing Department, Penguin Books Australia Ltd, P.O. Box 257, Ringwood, Victoria 3134.

In New Zealand: For a complete list of books available from Penguins in New Zealand write to the Marketing Department, Penguin Books (N.Z.) Ltd, Private Bag, Takapuna, Auckland 9.

In India: For a complete list of books available from Penguins in India write to Penguin Overseas Ltd, 706 Eros Apartments, 56 Nehru Place, New Delhi 110019.